Cupboard

STORIES WORLDWIDE

Fifty-Fifty Tutti-Frutti Chocolate-Chip

AND OTHER STORIES

EDITED BY ESTHER MENON

Heinemann
New Windmills

Heinemann Educational Publishers
Halley Court, Jordan Hill, Oxford OX2 8EJ
Part of Harcourt Education

Heinemann is the registered trademark of Harcourt Educational Limited

Selection, introduction and activities © Esther Menon, 2001

04 03
10 9 8 7 6 5 4 3

ISBN 0 435 12537 0

'Mr. Mongoose and Mrs. Hen' from *The Future Telling Lady and other stories* by James Berry, © James Berry; reprinted with permission of Peters Fraser & Dunlop Group Ltd. 'Attila' from *Malgudi Days* by R.K. Narayan, published by Penguin Books Ltd, © 1947, 1972 by R.K. Narayan; used by permission of the Wallace Literary Agency, Inc. 'First Foot' by Janice Galloway; reprinted with permission of A.P. Watt Ltd. 'The Vanishing Hitchhiker' from *Now That's What I Call Urban Myths* by Phil Healey and Rick Glanvill, published by Virgin Publishing, 1996; reprinted with permission of Virgin Publishing Ltd. 'The Sniper' by Liam O'Flaherty, © Liam O'Flaherty; reprinted by permission of Peters Fraser & Dunlop Ltd, on behalf of The Estate of Liam O'Flaherty. 'The Friendship' by Mildred D. Taylor, text © 1987 by Mildred D. Taylor; used by permission of Dial Books for Young Readers, an imprint of Penguin Putnam Books for Young Readers, a division of Penguin Putnam Inc. 'The Mirror' by Eiko Kadono; reprinted with permission of Japan Foreign-Rights Centre. 'Once Upon a Time' from *Jump and other stories* by Nadine Gordimer; reprinted with permission of A.P. Watt Ltd. 'The First of My Sins' by Brian Friel, from *Great Irish Stories of Childhood* by Peter Haining, published by Souvenir Press in 1997 © Brian Friel; reprinted with permission of Anthony Harwood Ltd, on behalf of the author. 'The Guest' by Leena Dhingra, from *Flaming Spirit*, edited by Ahmad and Gupta, published by Virago Press, 1994; reprinted with permission of the author. 'Fifty-Fifty Tutti-Frutti Chocolate Chip' by Norman Silver, from *An Eye for Colour*, published by Faber and Faber Ltd, © Norman Silver 1991; reprinted with permission of Laura Cecil Literary Agency, on behalf of the author. 'Two Kinda Truth' by Farrukh Dhondy, from *Come to Mecca and Other Stories*, published by HarperCollins Publishers, 1978, reprinted with permission of David Higham Associates Ltd.

Cover design by The Point
Cover illustration by Sue Williams
Illustrations by Jackie Hill at 320 Design: 'The Loaded Dog' – John Holder; 'Atilla' – John Holder; 'Sredni Vashtar' – Alan Baker; 'The Sniper' – Hashim Akib; 'Once Upon a Time' – Hashim Akib; 'The First of my Sins' – Kim Harley: 'The Guest' – Hashim Akib; 'Two Kinda Truth' – Andy Ward
Typeset by ⌐ Tek-Art, Croydon, Surrey
Printed in the UK by Clays Ltd, St Ives plc

Contents

With thanks to Alan Pearce,
Head of English, Buckler's Mead
School, Somerset, for his
comments and feedback in the
development of this anthology.

Introduction for students

In choosing these stories I have looked for really good stories that you will enjoy reading rather than just stories set in other countries and cultures. In today's world few countries have remained closed to wider cultures, and certainly Britain benefits from a rich variety of people, music, fashions, religions and foods. This book contains stories from around the world. Some deal with issues or traditions particular to an area, and some address issues that are shared across cultures, from England to South Africa, India to Ireland. Overall, you will find stories that show that the concerns of human beings are generally common ones. You will find stories that are funny, shocking, violent and heart-warming, but all, I hope, will offer situations you can identify with.

There is something here for everyone. For those of you who enjoy fun and humour, try *The Loaded Dog*. If you like thinking about the modern family, you will enjoy *The Mirror* and *First Foot*. For those of you interested in war and conflict, look at Liam O'Flaherty's *The Sniper* or *Once Upon a Time* by Nadine Gordimer. Many people now have their family roots in more than one culture and, if that interests you, look at the tension between cultures in Leena Dhingra's story *The Guest* or Farrukh Dhondy's *Two Kinda Truth*. As the writer Meera Syal has said, 'culture evolves and changes, just like human beings'. The younger generation can change things, and redefine what their own culture means, without losing pride in their roots. I hope not only that you will enjoy these stories but also that they will make you think about the part you play in the cultures that surround you.

Esther Menon

Introduction for teachers

One of the main challenges for English teachers in teaching literature from around the world is finding suitable and appealing resources, as opposed to finding classroom materials that merely meet syllabus criteria. The aim in putting together this anthology has been to select stories that Key Stage 3 students will find gripping, and that will encourage them to become 'enthusiastic, discriminating and responsive readers'. There are lively and macabre twists to the tales, unusual and problematic friendships across racial boundaries, teenage perspectives on the family and culture, and the violence of racism and war.

The stories in this book have been chosen for their appeal to young people rather than selected solely on the basis of their cultural origin. Experience with my own students has shown that many tend to avoid books set in cultures widely different from their own. The Activities certainly require students to consider the distinctive qualities of literature from various cultures. However, these stories will allow us as teachers to challenge the notion of 'otherness' and 'difference' in terms of culture, and consider the many links between the range of cultures represented here. The issues address worldwide and human concerns, though the language and settings offer much possibility for cultural analysis.

Though many of the stories can be linked together, I have avoided a prescriptive list of paired stories in the knowledge that teachers will want to use the materials in different ways for different groups of students. The chart on pages 198–199 summarises the links between the stories in terms of plot, structure, language and themes.

At the back of the book you will find extended writing activities that explicitly link pairs of stories together.

The stories in the book become progressively more difficult, from those that would be most appropriate for Year 7 students such as *Mr Mongoose and Mrs Hen* and *The Loaded Dog* to those that will move students at Year 9 towards GCSE such as *Fifty-Fifty Tutti-Frutti Chocolate-Chip* and *Two Kinda Truth*. This allows for differentiated group reading for whole-class teaching and the use of stories from a variety of cultures throughout KS3, in preparation for syllabus demands at KS4. Naturally some of the language and content in these texts is challenging, either academically or emotionally, for KS3 students. Most of them are appropriate for individual reading, though there are some, such as those by Norman Silver, Mildred D. Taylor and Farrukh Dhondy, that I would suggest are read in class to allow the teacher to qualify and discuss some of the more complex issues. The white boy's use of the word 'coon' in *Fifty-Fifty Tutti-Frutti Chocolate-Chip* is an example of language that my own students found problematic when trying to sympathise with him. Similarly, the violence of the action in Mildred D. Taylor's award-winning story *The Friendship* might be best dealt with in a whole-class situation.

Each story begins with some background notes for the students and a point for them to consider as they read through the text. The related Activities at the back of the book offer questions to develop reading and understanding, followed by reading, writing or speaking and listening activities linked to the text.

Esther Menon

Mr Mongoose and Mrs Hen
James Berry

This story is based on one that James Berry heard when he was a child. He later found out that it was originally an American folktale which had travelled to Jamaica. James Berry's disturbing version reads like a simple children's tale, but it is far more than that. The writer is using a technique called allegory. This means that he uses characters or events to stand for major ideas, so that the surface story has a deeper, more significant, meaning.

As you read, *think carefully about how the content relates to situations you might have come across in the modern world. Try to think of one word that summarises the topic of the story. Once you have finished reading, you might like to write this down and then discuss your opinion with others in the class.*

Mrs Hen was happy, six fluffy and beautiful chickens had come under her, and all about between her feathers, after three weeks of sitting on her nest. Out in the big yard for the first time, a proud mother, her six chicks peep-peeped around her. Mrs Hen clucked all the time, protectively, caringly, happily, every chick close to her. But, O, unhappiness waited for her. Though the last idea Mrs Hen would ever have was that somebody was somewhere all ready to turn her happiness into misery.

That Mr Mongoose peeped through the fence and saw Mrs Hen with her new chickens. And Mr Mongoose weighed everything up. Mr Mongoose looked to see who was about. Mr Mongoose hid himself and waited for everything to be exactly the right moment.

There in her yard, Mrs Hen was totally taken up with mothering her fluffy first-day chicks. Mrs Hen searched and clucked, calling her chicks to hurry and see who'd be the first to take any bits of food she'd found.

Mr Mongoose, careful not to be seen, strolled up into the yard as if he knew nothing would stop him. Then, with one straight reckless dash, Mr Mongoose charged right into the middle of Mrs Hen and chickens. Everything feathers and panic and terror, mother and chicks hollered and scattered, screaming. Nippily, cockily, as Mr Mongoose came, he left again. Vanished! Was gone! Shattered and stunned as she was, Mrs Hen turned here, turned there, calling her chicks together. In her terror, Mrs Hen moved quickly to the other side of her yard, with frightened chicks trying to keep up close beside her.

Mrs Hen comforted her chicks. She sat down. She got the chicks to nestle safely all around in her tummy feathers. But, clucking, clucking, calling, Mrs Hen knew one chick was missing. She knew – oh she knew – Mr Mongoose had gone off with one of her babies. Yet she couldn't stop calling. And that sound – that sound of Mrs Hen's calling – was the sad sound of a distressed mother.

Unexpectedly a voice spoke to Mrs Hen. 'Awful, isn't it? I know. I know how terrible it is.'

'You do?' Mrs Hen said, looking up and seeing Mrs Ground-Dove sitting on a low branch. 'I'm shattered,' Mrs Hen went on. 'Shattered. Thank you for saying something. Thank you so much.'

'I saw it all,' Mrs Ground-Dove said.

'You saw it happen?'

'I saw it happen.'

'What then can I do? Oh, what can I do?'

'Nothing.' Mrs Ground-Dove said.

Alarmed, Mrs Hen said, 'Nothing? Nothing I can do?'

'Nothing,' Mrs Ground-Dove said. 'I lost my whole family to that beast Mr Mongoose.'

'Your whole family?' Mrs Hen gasped.

'My whole, whole, family,' Mrs Ground-Dove said, 'And I tell you, I myself have to be careful. Have to be very careful. He's taken friends of mine. Taken them! And tried after me, too. Tried to turn me into feathers. Yes, he's tried.'

'This is dreadful,' Mrs Hen said. 'Dreadful. Do – do – if you hear, hear about anything – anything – that can be done, let me know. Please.'

'I will, I will,' Mrs Ground-Dove said and flew away.

Next morning Mrs Hen made sure she didn't take her babies to the same side of the fence as yesterday. But soon, so taken up in finding little extras for her chicks to eat, Mrs Hen found herself and family charged into again. Leaping into the air, Mrs Hen came down with wings flapping, ready for a fight, but Mr Mongoose was gone. Crying chickens were scattered everywhere. In her own state of terror, Mrs Hen collected her babies together behind her and again hurried away from the spot of attack.

Her chickens were under her, comforted between her feathers. But Mrs Hen clucked anxiously, knowing she'd lost another chick. Yet, worse was to happen.

In all, for six days, every day, Mr Mongoose strolled into the yard and carried off and ate one of Mrs Hen's chickens.

On that awful final morning when her last baby had been carried off, Mrs Hen was thrown into a kind of madness. Her hurt was more than a terrible sadness, for herself and for the pain of her lost chicks. Her loneliness was strange and peculiar. Without her chickens, the last one gone, it was as if she couldn't see, feel or hear anything and didn't know how to be herself. She found herself going about the yard, clucking, calling. Then she found herself searching for her old nest. Mrs Hen came to it and stood over it, looking in. She stepped into the old nest and sat down. Empty of eggs, empty of chicks, the nest was peculiar. It offered no peace, no comfort. All silly and miserable, Mrs Hen gave up the sitting and walked about the yard, clucking, calling, wishing for a miracle that'd make her chickens appear.

A voice came from nowhere. 'So, you're like me now,' it said.

Mrs Hen looked up and saw Mrs Ground-Dove on a low tree branch. 'Yes,' she replied. 'I'm like you now. My whole family! My whole family! I've lost my whole, whole family . . . What can I do? What can I do?'

'You could take that beast Mr Mongoose to court,' Mrs Ground-Dove said. 'You could take him to court.'

Mrs Hen looked away in great, great surprise and wonder. She'd never thought of taking Mr Mongoose to court. 'Yes,' she whispered. 'Yes! That *is* something I can do. That really *is* something.'

'It is, isn't it?' Mrs Ground-Dove said. 'I'll watch for the outcome. Good luck.'

Mrs Hen took Mr Mongoose to court.

Mr Mongoose was escorted by a policeman into court. Mrs Hen's charges against him were to do with attack, robbery and murder of her six baby chicks.

Mrs Hen sat waiting for the trial to begin. She was all

excited inside. She wanted to make sure she told what happened clearly and properly. She was getting everything orderly and clear in her head, when something struck her. Mrs Hen noticed that every policeman in court was a Mongoose. The clerk of the courts was a Mr Mongoose. The prosecutor was a Mr Mongoose. And the judge – the judge who'd just come in and sat down – was an older and big-bellied Mr Mongoose. Every official who ran the court was a Mr Mongoose! Mrs Hen was shocked, horrified, panic-stricken. She'd never felt more ganged-up against, more exposed, more tricked! Mrs Hen's shock and worry turned into a tight pain across her tummy. Mrs Hen wanted to talk to somebody official. She wanted to talk to somebody!

Mrs Hen pulled herself together, telling herself not to be silly. This was a court of law. It didn't matter who the officials were. It didn't matter one bit who the officials were.

Then, as if everything happened far, far away, Mrs Hen heard the officials of the court using her name a lot. The court was actually in session. Her case had started.

At last it was Mrs Hen's turn to tell her case against Mr Mongoose. She told the court how Mr Mongoose attacked her and her family and robbed her of all her baby chicks. Every day for six days Mr Mongoose came and took away one of her baby chickens. He took all of the six she had. That same Mr Mongoose standing there in court robbed her badly, brutally, and murdered her babies. And not one was left with her. Not one. And she was heartbroken and sad. She was asking the court to let Mr Mongoose repay her for the loss of her family, for their suffering, and for her suffering. And she was asking the court to punish Mr Mongoose. And to stop him from making any such attack on her or on anyone else ever, ever, again.

The court listened to Mrs Hen patiently. The court listened to her till she was completely finished.

Then one Mr Mongoose court official in a gown got up and spoke. And O the Mr Mongoose court official in his gown broke up Mrs Hen's story badly. He broke up her story and changed it badly, badly. And from then on every other Mr Mongoose court official talked about only the broken-up and changed story. And the same Mr Mongoose in the gown began to laugh, saying, 'My good lady, Mrs Hen, how can you actually bring a case like this to court against someone without proof? Without any proof whatsoever!'

'I hope you understand your case, Mrs Hen,' the Mr Mongoose judge said. 'You have no evidence. You have no witnesses to prove that what you accuse Mr Mongoose of is true. You have no witnesses. Do you understand that?'

Mrs Hen did not understand. But she didn't answer. She was too, too shocked and bewildered with disbelief at what she saw the judgment would be. And, truly, Mrs Hen lost her case.

Alone again, Mrs Hen started walking home.

Mrs Hen walked slowly across a field. Dazed, hardly able to move, she walked slowly on and on. Sad, sad, Mrs Hen's loneliness made her feel she walked in deepest darkness in a tunnel underground. And she carried the weight of the world. Her body was weighed-down, awkward, heavy. She could hardly walk. Really, it was her sadness that gripped her. Her sadness held her full of tears that would not come. Her head felt all a-spin. And the same thoughts went round and round: 'Cruelty . . . ! Dishonesty and cruelty . . . I'm lost . . . Lost . . . Mongooses have all the say. All the authority. It makes all mongooses say, yes! yes! yes! It makes them feel strong being dishonest and cruel. Their strength's their cruelty and self-deceit – all wrapped, well wrapped, in a pretence that looks like shining respectability . . . Cruelty crushes me. O – cruelty crushes you . . . And I have no more words . . . I'm lost . . . Lost . . .'

Unexpectedly, under a tree, a Mr Mongoose stood in front of Mrs Hen. Swiftly, Mrs Hen was surrounded by one, two, three, four Mr Mongooses. Everything about them was menacing. Every move and look on their faces was set with violence, attack, death. As they were closing in, Mrs Hen looked straight at one of the Mr Mongooses. She whispered, 'But, today – you – you were my judge!'

All four Mr Mongooses held Mrs Hen. They gripped her tight and hard. They killed Mrs Hen. And with noisy celebration, the four Mr Mongooses ate Mrs Hen.

The Loaded Dog
Henry Lawson

Henry Lawson is known for his short stories and ballads about the Australian outback. His stories are often very funny and the comedy in this tale is no exception.

As you read, *consider how the descriptions of the setting give clues to its Australian background. Write down any words that you think help to convey this.*

Dave Regan, Jim Bently and Andy Page were sinking a shaft at Stony Creek in search of a rich **gold quartz reef** which was supposed to exist in the **vicinity**. There is always a rich reef supposed to exist in the vicinity; the only questions are whether it is ten feet or hundreds beneath the surface, and in which direction. They had struck some pretty solid rock, also water which kept them bailing. They used the old-fashioned blasting-powder and time-fuse. They'd make a sausage or cartridge of blasting-powder in a skin of strong **calico** or canvas, the mouth sewn and bound round the end of the fuse; they'd dip the cartridge in melted **tallow** to make it watertight, get the drill-hole as dry as possible, drop in the cartridge with some dry dust, and wad and

---

gold quartz: gold-bearing mineral
reef: vein or seam of mineral
vicinity: neighbourhood
calico: cotton cloth
tallow: mutton fat

ram with stiff clay and broken brick. Then they'd light the fuse and get out of the hole and wait. The result was usually an ugly pot-hole in the bottom of the shaft and half a barrow-load of broken rock.

There was plenty of fish in the creek, fresh-water bream, cod, cat-fish and tailers. The party were fond of fish, and Andy and Dave of fishing. Andy would fish for three hours at a stretch if encouraged by a nibble or a bite now and then – say once in twenty minutes. The butcher was always willing to give meat in exchange for fish when they caught more than they could eat; but now it was winter, and these fish wouldn't bite. However, the creek was low, just a chain of muddy waterholes, from the hole with a few bucketfuls in it to the sizeable pool with an average depth of six or seven feet, and they could get fish by bailing out the smaller holes or muddying up the water in the larger ones till the fish rose to the surface. There was the cat-fish, with spikes growing out of the sides of its head, and if you got pricked you'd know it, as Dave said. Andy took off his boots, tucked up his trousers, and went into a hole one day to stir up the mud with his feet, and he knew it. Dave scooped one out with his hand and got pricked, and he knew it too; his arm swelled, and the pain throbbed up into his shoulder, and down into his stomach, too, he said, like a toothache he had once, and kept him awake for two nights – only the toothache pain had a 'burred edge', Dave said.

Dave got an idea.

'Why not blow the fish up in the big waterhole with a cartridge?' he said. 'I'll try it.'

He thought the thing out and Andy Page worked it out. Andy usually put Dave's theories into practice if they were practicable, or bore the blame for the failure and **chaffing** of his mates if they weren't.

He made a cartridge about three times the size of those they used in the rock. Jim Bently said it was big enough to blow the bottom out of the river. The inner skin was of stout calico; Andy stuck the end of a six-foot piece of fuse well down in the powder and bound the mouth of the bag firmly to it with whipcord. The idea was to sink the cartridge in the water with the open end of the fuse attached to a float on the surface, ready for lighting. Andy dipped the cartridge in melted beeswax to make it watertight. 'We'll have to leave it some time before we light it,' said Dave, 'to give the fish time to get over their scare when we put it in, and come nosing round again; so we'll want it well watertight.'

Round the cartridge Andy, at Dave's suggestion, bound a strip of sail canvas – that they used for making water-bags – to increase the force of the explosion, and round that he pasted layers of stiff brown paper – on the plan of the sort of fireworks we called 'gun-crackers'. He let the paper dry in the sun, then he sewed a covering of two thicknesses of canvas over it, and bound the thing from end to end with stout fishing-line. Dave's schemes were elaborate, and he often worked his inventions out to nothing. The cartridge was rigid and solid enough now – a formidable bomb; but Andy and Dave wanted to be sure. Andy sewed on another layer of canvas, dipped the cartridge in melted tallow, twisted a length of fencing-wire round it as an afterthought, dipped it in

chaffing: teasing

tallow again, and stood it carefully against a tent-peg, where he'd know where to find it, and wound the fuse loosely round it. Then he went to the camp-fire to try some potatoes which were boiling in their jackets in a **billy**, and to see about frying some chops for dinner. Dave and Jim were at work in the claim that morning.

They had a big, black, young retriever dog – or rather an overgrown pup, a big, foolish, four-footed mate, who was always slobbering round them and lashing their legs with his heavy tail that swung round like a stockwhip. Most of his head was usually a red, idiotic slobbering grin of appreciation of his own silliness. He seemed to take life, the world, his two-legged mates, and his own instinct as a huge joke. He'd retrieve anything; he carted back most of the camp rubbish that Andy threw away. They had a cat that died in hot weather, and Andy threw it a good distance away in the **scrub**; and early one morning the dog found the cat, after it had been dead a week or so, and carried it back to camp, and laid it just inside the tent-flaps, where it could best make its presence known when the mates should rise and begin to sniff suspiciously in the sickly smothering atmosphere of the summer sunrise. He used to retrieve them when they went in swimming; he'd jump in after them, and scratch their naked bodies with his paws. They loved him for his good-heartedness and his foolishness, but when they wished to enjoy a swim they had to tie him up in camp.

He watched Andy with great interest all the morning making the cartridge, and hindered him considerably,

---

billy: metal pan or kettle
scrub: rough vegetation

trying to help; but about noon he went off to the claim to see how Dave and Jim were getting on, and to come home to dinner with them. Andy saw them coming, and put a panful of mutton-chops on the fire. Andy was cook today; Dave and Jim stood with their backs to the fire, as bushmen do in all weathers, waiting till dinner should be ready. The retriever went nosing round after something he seemed to have missed.

Andy's brain still worked on the cartridge; his eye was caught by the glare of an empty **kerosene**-tin lying in the bushes, and it struck him that it wouldn't be a bad idea to sink the cartridge packed with clay, sand or stones in the tin, to increase the force of the explosion. He may have been all out, from a scientific point of view, but the notion looked all right to him. Jim Bently, by the way, wasn't interested in their 'damned silliness'. Andy noticed an empty treacle-tin – the sort with the little tin neck or spout soldered on to the top for the convenience of pouring out the treacle – and it struck him that this would have made the best kind of cartridge-case: he would only have had to pour in the powder, stick the fuse in through the neck, and cork and seal it with beeswax. He was turning to suggest this to Dave, when Dave glanced over his shoulder to see how the chops were doing – and bolted. He explained afterwards that he thought he heard the pan spluttering extra, and looked to see if the chops were burning. Jim Bently looked behind and bolted after Dave. Andy stood stock-still, staring after them.

'Run, Andy! Run!' they shouted back at him. 'Run! Look behind you, you fool! Andy turned slowly and

---

kerosene: paraffin oil, used for heating and lighting

looked, and there, close behind him, was the retriever with the cartridge in his mouth – wedged into his broadest and silliest grin. And that wasn't all. The dog had come round the fire to Andy, and the loose end of the fuse had trailed and waggled over the burning sticks into the blaze; Andy had slit and nicked the firing end of the fuse well, and now it was hissing and spitting properly.

Andy's legs started with a jolt; his legs started before his brain did, and he made after Dave and Jim. And the dog followed Andy.

Dave and Jim were good runners – Jim the best – for a short distance; Andy was slow and heavy, but he had the strength and the wind and could last. The dog capered round him, delighted as a dog could be to find

his mates, as he thought, on for a frolic. Dave and Jim kept shouting back, 'Don't foller us! Don't foller us, you coloured fool!' But Andy kept on, no matter how they dodged. They could never explain, any more than the dog, why they followed each other, but so they ran, Dave keeping in Jim's track in all its turnings, Andy after Dave, and the dog circling round Andy – the live fuse swishing in all directions and hissing and spluttering and stinking. Jim yelling to Dave not to follow him, Dave shouting to Andy to go in another direction – to 'spread out' – and Andy roaring at the dog to go home. Then Andy's brain began to work, stimulated by the crisis: he tried to get a running kick at the dog, but the dog dodged; he snatched up sticks and stones and threw them at the dog and ran on again. The retriever saw that he'd made a mistake about Andy, and left him and bounded after Dave. Dave, who had the presence of mind to think that the fuse's time wasn't up yet, made a dive and a grab for the dog, caught him by the tail, and as he swung round snatched the cartridge out of his mouth and flung it as far as he could; the dog immediately bounded after it and retrieved it. Dave roared and cursed at the dog, who, seeing that Dave was offended left him and went after Jim, who was well ahead. Jim swung to a sapling and went up it like a native bear; it was a young sapling, and Jim couldn't safely get more than ten or twelve feet from the ground. The dog laid the cartridge, as carefully as if it were a kitten, at the foot of the sapling, and capered and leaped and whooped joyously round under Jim. The big pup reckoned that this was part of the lark – he was all right now – it was Jim who was out for a spree. The fuse sounded as if it were going a mile a minute. Jim tried to climb higher and the sapling bent and cracked. Jim fell on his feet and ran. The dog swooped on the cartridge and followed. It all took but a very few moments. Jim ran to a digger's hole, about ten feet deep, and dropped down into it – landing on soft mud – and was safe. The dog grinned **sardonically** down at him, over the edge, for a moment, as if he thought it would be a good lark to drop the cartridge down on Jim.

'Go away, Tommy,' said Jim feebly, 'go away.'

The dog bounded off after Dave, who was the only one in sight now; Andy had dropped behind a log, where he lay flat on his face, having suddenly remembered a picture of the Russo-Turkish war with a circle of Turks lying flat on their faces (as if they were ashamed) round a newly-arrived shell.

There was a small hotel or **shanty** on the creek, on the main road, not far from the claim. Dave was desperate, and time flew much faster in his stimulated imagination than it did in reality, so he made for the shanty. There were several casual **bushmen** on the veranda and in the bar; Dave rushed into the bar, banging the door to behind him. 'My dog!' he gasped, in reply to the astonished stare of the publican, 'the blanky retriever – he's got a live cartridge in his mouth –'

The retriever, finding the front door shut against him, had bounded round and in by the back way, and now stood smiling in the doorway leading from the passage,

---

sardonically: humourlessly
shanty: roughly-built cabin
bushmen: Australians who live or travel in the wilderness

the cartridge still in his mouth and the fuse spluttering. They burst out of that bar; Tommy bounded first after one and then after another, for, being a young dog, he tried to make friends with everybody.

The bushmen ran round corners, and some shut themselves in the stable. There was a new weatherboard and corrugated-iron kitchen and wash-house on piles in the backyard, with some women washing clothes inside. Dave and the publican bundled in there and shut the door – the publican cursing Dave and calling him a crimson fool, in hurried tones, and wanting to know what the hell he came here for.

The retriever went in under the kitchen, amongst the piles, but, luckily for those inside, there was a vicious yellow mongrel cattle-dog sulking and nursing his nastiness under there – a sneaking, fighting, thieving canine, whom neighbours had tried for years to shoot or poison. Tommy saw his danger – he'd had experience from this dog – and started out and across the yard, still sticking to the cartridge. Half-way across the yard the yellow dog caught him and nipped him. Tommy dropped the cartridge, gave one terrified yell, and took to the bush. The yellow dog followed him to the fence and then ran back to see what he had dropped. Nearly a dozen other dogs came from round all the corners and under the buildings – spidery, thievish, cold-blooded kangaroo-dogs, mongrel sheep- and cattle-dogs, vicious black and yellow dogs – that slip after you in the dark, nip your heels, and vanish without explaining – and yapping, yelping small fry. They kept at a respectable distance round the nasty yellow dog, for it was dangerous to go near him when he thought he had found something which might be good for a dog or cat. He sniffed at the cartridge twice, and was just taking a third cautious sniff when –

It was a very good blasting-powder – a new brand that Dave had recently got up from Sydney; and the cartridge had been excellently well made. Andy very patient and painstaking in all he did, and nearly as handy as the average sailor with needles, twine, canvas and rope.

Bushmen say that the kitchen jumped off its piles and on again. When the smoke and dust cleared away, the remains of the nasty yellow dog were lying against the paling fence of the yard looking as if it had been kicked into a fire by a horse and afterwards rolled in the dust under a barrow, and finally thrown against the fence from a distance. Several saddle-horses, which had been 'hanging-up' round the veranda, were galloping wildly down the road in clouds of dust, with broken bridle-reins flying; and from a circle round the outskirts, from every point of the compass in the scrub, came the yelping of dogs. Two of them went home, to the place where they were born, thirty miles away, and reached it the same night and stayed there; it was not till towards evening that the rest came back cautiously to make inquiries. One was trying to walk on two legs, and most of 'em looked more or less singed; and a little, singed, stumpy-dog, who had been in the habit of hopping the back half of him along on one leg, had reason to be glad that he'd saved up the other leg all those years, for he needed it now. There was one old one-eyed cattle-dog round that shanty for years afterwards, who couldn't stand the smell of a gun being cleaned. He it was who had taken an interest, only second to that of the yellow dog, in the cartridge.

Bushmen said that it was amusing to slip up on his blind side and stick a dirty **ramrod** under his nose: he wouldn't wait to bring his solitary eye to bear – he'd take to the bush and stay out all night.

For half an hour or so after the explosion there were several bushmen round behind the stable who crouched, doubled up, against the wall, or rolled gently on the dust, trying to laugh without shrieking. There were two white women in hysterics at the house, and a half-caste rushing aimlessly round with a dipper of cold water. The publican was holding his wife tight and begging her between her squawks, to 'Hold up for my sake, Mary, or I'll lam the life out of ye!'

Dave decided to apologise later on, 'when things had settled a bit', and went back to camp. And the dog that had done it all, Tommy, the great, idiotic mongrel retriever, came slobbering round Dave and lashing his legs with his tail, and trotted home after him, smiling his broadest, longest and reddest smile of **amiability**, and apparently satisfied for one afternoon with the fun he'd had.

Andy chained the dog up securely, and cooked some more chops, while Dave went to help Jim out of the hole.

And most of this is why, for years afterwards, lanky, easy-going bushmen, riding lazily past Dave's camp, would cry, in a lazy drawl and with just a hint of the nasal twang:

''Ello, Da-a-ve! How's the fishin' getting on, Da-a-ve?'

---

ramrod: rod for cleaning the barrel of a gun
amiability: friendliness

Attila

R.K. Narayan

This story is set in India and describes a dog that does not live up to its name. It is written by the famous South Indian writer R.K. Narayan, who is well known for lively and comical observation of human behaviour. In this story Narayan describes the common situation of children being loyal to their pets and the more realistic attitude of parents.

As you read, *think carefully about how the writer creates comedy by showing various points of view in the story: the mother's, the son's, Ranga's and Attila's own.*

In a mood of optimism they named him '**Attila**'. What they wanted of a dog was strength, formidableness and fight, and **hence** he was named after the 'Scourge of Europe'.

The puppy was only a couple of months old; he had square jaws, red eyes, a pug nose and a massive head, and there was every reason to hope that he would do credit to his name. The immediate reason for buying him was a series of house-breakings and thefts in the neighbourhood, and our householders decided to put more trust in a dog than in the police. They searched far and wide and met a dog fancier. He held

---

Attila: Attila the Hun, the most successful of the barbarian invaders of the Roman Empire
hence: so

up a month-old black-and-white puppy and said, 'Come and fetch him a month **hence**. In six months he will be something to be feared and respected.' He spread out before them a pedigree sheet which was stunning. The puppy had running in his veins the choicest and the most ferocious blood.

They were satisfied, paid an advance, returned a month later, put down seventy-five **rupees** and took the puppy home. The puppy, as I have already indicated, did not have a very **prepossessing** appearance and was none too playful, but this did not prevent his owners from sitting in a circle around him and admiring him. There was a prolonged debate as to what he should be named. The youngest suggested, 'Why not call him Tiger?'

'Every other street-mongrel is named Tiger,' came the reply. 'Why not Caesar?'

'Caesar! If a **census** was taken of dogs you would find at least fifteen thousand Caesars in South India alone . . . Why not Fire?'

'It is fantastic.'

'Why not Thunder?'

'It is too obvious.'

'Grip?'

'Still obvious, and childish.'

There was a **deadlock**. Someone suggested Attila, and a shout of joy went up to the skies. No more satisfying name was thought of for man or animal.

---

hence: from now
rupees: Indian money
prepossessing: attractive
census: count
deadlock: standstill

But as time passed our Attila exhibited a love of humanity which was sometimes disconcerting. The Scourge of Europe – could he ever have been like this? They put it down to his age. What child could help loving all creatures? In their **zeal** to establish this fact, they went to the extent of delving into ancient history to find out what the Scourge of Europe was like when he was a child. It was rumoured that as a child he clung to his friends and to his parents' friends so fast that often he had to be beaten and separated from them. But when he was fourteen he showed the first sign of his future: he knocked down and plunged his knife into a fellow who tried to touch his marbles. Ah, this was encouraging. Let our dog reach the parallel of fourteen years and people would get to know his real nature.

But this was a vain promise. He stood up twenty inches high, had a large frame and a forbidding appearance on the whole – but that was all. A variety of people entered the gates of the house every day: **mendicants**, bill-collectors, postmen, tradesmen and family friends. All of them were warmly received by Attila. The moment the gate clicked he became alert and stood up looking towards the gate. By the time anyone entered the gate Attila went blindly charging forward. But that was all. The person had only to stop and smile, and Attila would melt. He would behave as if he apologised for even giving an impression of violence. He would lower his head, curve his body, tuck his tail between his legs, roll his eyes and moan as

---

zeal: enthusiasm
mendicants: beggars

if to say, 'How sad that you should have mistaken my gesture! I only hurried down to greet you.' Till he was patted on the head, stroked and told that he was forgiven, he would be in extreme misery.

Gradually he realised that his bouncing advances caused much unhappy misunderstanding. And so when he heard the gate click he hardly stirred. He merely looked in that direction and wagged his tail. The people at home did not like this attitude very much. They thought it rather a shame.

'Why not change his name to Blind Worm?' somebody asked.

'He eats like an elephant,' said the mother of the family.

'You can employ two watchmen for the price of the rice and meat he consumes. Somebody comes every

morning and steals all the flowers in the garden and Attila won't do anything about it.'

'He has better business to do than catch flower thieves,' replied the youngest, always the defender of the dog.

'What is the better business?'

'Well, if somebody comes in at dawn and takes away the flowers, do you expect Attila to be looking out for him even at that hour?'

'Why not? It's what a well-fed dog ought to be doing instead of sleeping. You ought to be ashamed of your dog.'

'He does not sleep all night, Mother. I have often seen him going round the house and watching all night.'

'Really! Does he prowl about all night?'

'Of course he does,' said the defender.

'I am quite alarmed to hear it,' said the mother. 'Please lock him up in a room at night, otherwise he may call in a burglar and show him around. Left alone, a burglar might after all be less successful. It wouldn't be so bad if he at least barked. He is the most noiseless dog I have ever seen in my life.'

The young man was extremely irritated at this. He considered it to be the most uncharitable **cynicism**, but the dog justified it that very night.

Ranga lived in a hut three miles from the town. He was a '**gang coolie**' – often employed in road-mending. Occasionally at night he enjoyed the thrill and profit of breaking into houses. At one o'clock that night Ranga removed the bars of a window on the eastern side of

---

cynicism: lack of faith
gang coolie: casual labourer

the house and slipped in. He edged along the wall, searched all the trunks and ***almirahs*** in the house and made a neat bundle of all the jewellery and other valuables he could pick up.

He was just starting to go out. He had just put one foot out of the gap he had made in the window when he saw Attila standing below, looking up expectantly. Ranga thought his end had come. He expected the dog to bark. But not Attila. He waited for a moment, grew tired of waiting, stood up and put his forepaws on the lap of the burglar. He put back his ears, licked Ranga's hands and rolled his eyes. Ranga whispered, 'I hope you aren't going to bark . . .'

'Don't you worry. I am not the sort,' the dog tried to say.

'Just a moment. Let me get down from here,' said the burglar.

The dog obligingly took away his paws and lowered himself.

'See there,' said Ranga, pointing to the back yard, 'there is a cat.' Attila put up his ears at the mention of a cat and dashed in the direction indicated. One might easily have thought he was going to tear up a cat, but actually he didn't want to miss the pleasure of the company of a cat if there was one.

As soon as the dog left him Ranga made a dash for the gate. Given a second more he would have hopped over it. But the dog turned and saw what was about to happen and in one spring was at the gate. He looked hurt. 'Is this proper?' he seemed to ask. 'Do you want to shake me off?'

---

almirahs: wardrobes

He hung his heavy tail down so loosely and looked so miserable that the burglar stroked his head, at which he revived. The burglar opened the gate and went out, and the dog followed him. Attila's greatest ambition in life was to wander in the streets freely. Now things seemed to be shaping up ideally.

Attila liked his new friend so much that he wouldn't leave him alone even for a moment. He lay before Ranga when he sat down to eat, sat on the edge of his mat when he slept in his hut, waited patiently on the edge of the pond when Ranga went there now and then for a wash, slept on the roadside when Ranga was at work.

This sort of companionship got on Ranga's nerves. He implored, 'Oh, dog. Leave me alone for a moment, won't you?' Unmoved, Attila sat before him with his eyes glued on his friend.

Attila's disappearance created a sensation in the bungalow. 'Didn't I tell you,' the mother said, 'to lock him up? Now some burglar has gone away with him. What a shame! We can hardly mention it to anyone.'

'You are mistaken,' replied the defender. 'It is just a coincidence. He must have gone off on his own account. If he had been here no thief would have dared to come in . . .'

'Whatever it is, I don't know if we should after all thank the thief for taking away that dog. He may keep the jewels as a reward for taking him away. Shall we withdraw the police complaint?'

This **facetiousness ceased** a week later, and Attila rose to the ranks of a hero. The eldest son of the house

---

facetiousness: joking
ceased: stopped

was going towards the market one day. He saw Attila trotting behind someone on the road.

'Hey,' shouted the young man; at which Ranga turned and broke into a run. Attila, who always suspected that his new friend was waiting for the slightest chance to desert him, galloped behind Ranga.

'Hey, Attila!' shouted the young man, and he also started running. Attila wanted to answer the call after making sure of his friend; and so he turned his head for a second and galloped faster. Ranga desperately doubled his pace. Attila determined to stick to him at any cost. As a result, he ran so fast that he overtook Ranga and clumsily blocked his way, and Ranga stumbled over him and fell. As he rolled on the ground a piece of jewellery (which he was taking to a receiver of stolen property) flew from his hand. The young man recognised it as belonging to his sister and sat down on Ranga. A crowd collected and the police appeared on the scene.

Attila was the hero of the day. Even the lady of the house softened towards him. She said 'Whatever one might say of Attila, one has to admit that he is a very cunning detective. He is too deep for words.'

It was as well that Attila had no powers of speech. Otherwise he would have burst into a **lamentation** which would have shattered the **pedestal** under his feet.

---

lamentation: crying
pedestal: stand or plinth for a statue

Sredni Vashtar
Saki (H.H. Munro)

Saki was the name used by Hector Hugh Munro when he became a full-time writer. He was a Scot, born in Burma, and was sent back to England when he was young and brought up by two very strict aunts. Saki is well known for his clever and often horrifying stories and this grisly tale is no exception. He was killed in World War One.

As you read, *think about the character of Conradin. What would you expect him to be like from the first line of the story and how does this fit in with what you learn of him as the story progresses?*

Conradin was ten and the doctor had pronounced that the boy would not live another five years. The doctor counted for little, but his opinion was **endorsed** by Mrs de Ropp, who counted for nearly everything. Mrs de Ropp was Conradin's cousin and guardian, and in his eyes she represented those three-fifths of the world that are necessary and disagreeable and real; the other two-fifths were summed up in himself and his imagination. Without his imagination, Conradin would have **succumbed** to Mrs de Ropp long ago.

Mrs de Ropp would never have confessed that she disliked Conradin, though **thwarting** him 'for his good'

---

endorsed: approved
succumbed: given in
thwarting: frustrating

was a duty which she did not find particularly **irksome**. Conradin hated her with a desperate sincerity which he was perfectly able to **mask**. Such few pleasures as he could **contrive** gained an added **relish** from the likelihood that they would be **displeasing** to his guardian, and from the realm of his imagination she was locked out – an unclean thing.

In the dull, cheerless garden, overlooked by so many windows that were ready to open with a message not to do this or that, or a reminder that medicines were due, he found little attraction. The few fruit trees were set jealously apart from his plucking, as though they were rare specimens; it would have been difficult to find a market-gardener who would have offered ten shillings for their entire produce. In a forgotten corner, however, almost hidden behind a dismal shrubbery, was a disused tool-shed, and within its walls Conradin found a **haven**. He had peopled it with a legion of familiar phantoms, **evoked** partly from history and partly from his own brain, but it also boasted two inmates of flesh and blood. In one corner lived a **ragged-plumaged** Houdan hen, on which the boy lavished an affection that had scarcely another outlet. Further back in the gloom stood a large hutch with

---

irksome: irritating
mask: hide
contrive: invent
relish: enjoyment
displeasing: annoying
haven: peaceful place
evoked: called up
ragged-plumaged: with scruffy feathers

iron bars, the **abode** of a large **polecat-ferret**, which a friendly butcher-boy had once smuggled in, cage and all, in exchange for a long-**secreted** hoard of small silver. Conradin was dreadfully afraid of the **lithe**, sharp-fanged beast, but it was his most treasured possession. Its very presence in the shed was a secret and fearful joy, to be kept **scrupulously** from the knowledge of the Woman, as he privately **dubbed** his cousin. And one day he spun the beast a wonderful

---

abode: home
polecat-ferret: large weasel-like animal
secreted: hidden
lithe: graceful
scrupulously: carefully
dubbed: called

name, and from that moment it grew into a god and a religion. The Woman indulged in religion once a week at a church near by, and took Conradin with her, but to him the church service was alien. Every Thursday, in the dim and **musty** silence of the tool-shed, he worshipped before the wooden hutch where dwelt Sredni Vashtar, the great ferret. Red flowers in their season and scarlet berries in the winter-time were offered at his shrine, for he was a god who laid some special stress on the fierce, impatient side of things, as opposed to the Woman's religion. And on great festivals, powdered nutmeg was **strewn** in front of his hutch, an important feature of the offering being that the nutmeg had to be stolen. These festivals were irregular, and were chiefly appointed to celebrate some passing event. When Mrs de Ropp suffered acute toothache for three days, Conradin kept up the festival during the entire three days, and almost succeeded in persuading himself that Sredni Vashtar was personally responsible for the toothache. If the **malady** had lasted for another day the supply of nutmeg would have given out.

The Houdan hen was never drawn into the **cult** of Sredni Vashtar. Conradin had long ago settled that she was an **Anabaptist**. He did not pretend to have the remotest knowledge as to what an Anabaptist was, but he privately hoped that it was dashing and not very respectable.

---

musty: damp-smelling
strewn: scattered
malady: illness
cult: religion
Anabaptist: someone who rejects the baptism of children

After a while, Conradin's **absorption** in the tool-shed began to attract the notice of his guardian. 'It is not good for him to be pottering down there in all weathers,' she promptly decided, and at breakfast one morning she announced that the Houdan hen had been sold and taken away overnight. With her short-sighted eyes she peered at Conradin, waiting for an outbreak of rage and sorrow, which she was ready to **rebuke**. But Conradin said nothing: there was nothing to be said. Something perhaps in his white set face gave her a **momentary qualm**, for at tea that afternoon there was toast on the table, a delicacy which she usually banned on the ground that it was bad for him; also because the making of it 'gave trouble', a deadly offence in the middle-class feminine eye.

'I thought you liked toast,' she exclaimed, with an injured air, observing that he did not touch it.

'Sometimes,' said Conradin.

In the shed that evening there was an **innovation** in the worship of the hutch-god. Conradin had been **wont to** chant his praises, tonight he asked a **boon**.

'Do one thing for me, Sredni Vashtar.'

The thing was not specified. As Sredni Vashtar was a god he must be supposed to know. And choking back a sob as he looked at that other empty corner, Conradin went back to the world he so hated.

---

absorption: extreme interest
rebuke: tell off
momentary qualm: passing feeling of uneasiness or regret
innovation: new development
wont to: in the habit of
boon: benefit, blessing

And every night, in the welcome darkness of his bedroom, and every evening in the dusk of the tool-shed, Conradin's bitter **litany** went up: 'Do one thing for me, Sredni Vashtar.'

Mrs de Ropp noticed that the visits to the shed did not cease, and one day she made a further journey of inspection.

'What are you keeping in that locked hutch?' she asked. 'I believe it's guinea-pigs. I'll have them all cleared away.'

Conradin shut his lips tight, but the Woman ransacked his bedroom till she found the carefully-hidden key, and forthwith marched down to the shed. It was a cold afternoon, and Conradin had been **bidden** to keep to the house. From the furthest window of the dining-room the door of the shed could just be seen beyond the corner of the shrubbery, and there Conradin **stationed** himself. He saw the Woman enter, and then he imagined her opening the door of the sacred hutch and peering down with her short-sighted eyes into the thick straw bed where his god lay hidden. Perhaps she would prod at the straw in her clumsy impatience. And Conradin **fervently** breathed his prayer for the last time. But he knew as he prayed that he did not believe. He knew that the Woman would come out presently with that **pursed** smile he loathed so well

---

litany: prayer
bidden: ordered
stationed: positioned
fervently: full of emotion
pursed: self-satisfied

on her face, and that in an hour or two the gardener would carry away his wonderful god, a god no longer, but a simple brown ferret in a hutch. And he knew that the Woman would triumph always as she triumphed now, and that he would grow ever more sickly under her pestering and **domineering** and superior wisdom, till one day nothing would matter much more with him, and the doctor would be proved right. And in the sting and misery of his defeat, he began to chant loudly and defiantly the hymn of his threatened idol:

> *Sredni Vashtar went forth,*
> *His thoughts were red thoughts and his teeth*
>   *were white.*
> *His enemies called for peace, but he brought*
>   *them death.*
> *Sredni Vashtar the Beautiful.*

And then of a sudden he stopped his chanting and drew closer to the window-pane. The door of the shed still stood ajar as it had been left, and the minutes were slipping by. They were long minutes, but they slipped by nevertheless. He watched the starlings running and flying in little parties across the lawn; he counted them over and over again, with one eye always on that swinging door. A sour-faced maid came in to lay the table for tea, and still Conradin stood and waited and watched. Hope had crept by inches into his heart, and now a look of triumph began to blaze in his eyes that had only

---

domineering: bossiness

known the **wistful** patience of defeat. Under his breath he began once again that **paean** of victory and devastation. And presently his eyes were rewarded: out through the doorway came a long, low, yellow-and-brown beast, with eyes a-blink at the waning daylight, and dark wet stains around the fur of jaws and throat. Conradin dropped on his knees. The great polecat-ferret made its way down to a small brook at the foot of the garden, drank for a moment then crossed a little plank-bridge and was lost to sight in the bushes. Such was the passing of Sredni Vashtar.

'Tea is ready,' said the sour-faced maid; 'where is the mistress?'

'She went down to the shed some time ago,' said Conradin.

And while the maid went to summon her mistress to tea, Conradin fished a toasting-fork out of the sideboard drawer and proceeded to toast himself a piece of bread. And during the toasting of it and the buttering of it with much butter and the slow enjoyment of eating it, Conradin listened to the noises and silences beyond the dining-room door. The loud foolish screaming of the maid, the answering chorus of wondering **ejaculations** from the kitchen region, the scuttering footsteps and hurried **embassies** for outside help, and then, after a lull, the scared sobbings and the shuffling tread of those who bore a heavy burden into the house.

---

wistful: sadly thoughtful
paean: song of triumph
ejaculations: exclamations
embassies: messengers

'Whoever will break it to the poor child? I couldn't for the life of me!' exclaimed a shrill voice. And while they debated the matter among themselves, Conradin made himself another piece of toast.

First Foot
Janice Galloway

This Scottish story is based around the tradition of First Foot, which happens at New Year in Scotland. The tradition is that the first visitor who enters a home after midnight on New Year's Eve brings a gift. The story is about a teenage girl and the difficulties she has at home. We see how she feels about her much older sister who bullies her, and how she would rather be out of the house with her friend. Still, New Year is about new starts, new resolutions and being thoughtful to others . . . maybe things will change.

As you read, *think about the narrator. Although her family might consider her a moody teenager, her account shows she appreciates a lot of things in life and knows what makes her happy. What are the things in life that she values and finds pleasure in?*

It was the sun nearly woke me this morning. One minute I'm asleep and the next I'm awake and staring at the clock. It says five to eight so I've had a good sleep. I'm lying back congratulating myself on it when I notice how light the room is, even through the curtains. First sunny day of the New Year, I think. Has to be a good sign.

I can still hear Mammy thumping about in the living-room, putting the divan up, transforming it with **sleight** of cushions into a settee again. I hold my breath

---

sleight: magic tricks

and listen, but there's still no telling what sort of mood she's in. It's a sort of neutral thumping about. I stretch out full, tipping the head-and-foot-board at once and grinning at the ceiling, then sling my legs over the edge of the bed to sit up, still listening. It does seem a wee bit more noisy than usual right enough. Taking a bit of a risk, I think. Maybe wake up the **gorgon**. And that decides it.

I hate being in when my sister gets up. We *don't get on*, that is to say we hate the sight of each other. I mean it too – we've both been working on it a long time, as far back as I can remember (and probably before that on her side). With me, it's fear. She hates me because she thinks everything I do is specially designed to get at her. For example, I don't smoke/she gets through forty a day; I wake up early/she sleeps till noon; I like peace and quiet/she likes perpetual telly. I'm sixteen. She's thirty-seven. I sometimes think that last bit is the **crux** of the whole thing. That, and my **passivity**. I'm really wet. When she hits me, she knows I won't hit her back and it makes her worse, like she thinks I'm trying to prove I'm better than her or something. And I'm not. Irene is unpredictable and vicious with it. I'm just scared sick.

On top of that, she hates mornings. She treats them with a fierce spite, and I'm not going to get in the way of that, not with the day being so nice as well. I'm going to get up and go for Joseph. Maybe go for a walk on the shore front, down the shops, buy a magazine. Just so long as it's out.

---

gorgon: female monster
crux: essential point
passivity: lack of resistance

So I get up and I go for a wash. As soon as I turn the taps on, Mammy shouts through for me not to use up all the hot water, then I hear her putting the kettle on to make me a cup of tea. I think about shouting back for her not to bother – but I don't mind. I'm safe enough for ten minutes or so anyway.

I put on the clothes still lying about the floor from the night before: saves me thinking and saves me getting a row about leaving the place a mess. I push the curtains to one side while I'm doing up my shirt and there's the sun. It really is glorious. One of those clear, nippy days right at the start of the year when you think you can see into the middle of next week and the colours are really sharp. **Wee** blades of grass out the back coated with frost and next-door's washing still on the line, totally stiff like cardboard. And there's this cartoon picture in my head, somebody sawing the washing off the line and bashing it with a hammer to fold it – just daft things making me laugh and the sky pure blue and completely cloudless.

Not much of a laughing mood in the kitchenette, though. Just Mammy standing at the window in her dressing-gown and slippers. She hands the mug over without looking at me. Then she says: 'It's you should be making me breakfast, never mind the other way round.'

She sometimes gets like that in the mornings, especially at holidays. Third of January already, but the **haar** of the New Year still hangs on round the house. She turns her back to clatter about making toast and things, muttering about ingratitude. It's the way she's

---

wee: small
haar: fog, mist

woken up, and I can feel my face miserable in spite of myself. I can't stay in with this, I think. It's going to get me down and I know what happens after that. I get myself into a depression and that makes Mammy worse and then Irene gets up out of her bed like the thing from the black lagoon . . . I'm for off while I've got the chance.

So I sneak on my duffel and get my bag. Quiet. It's always important not to give the game away that I know what's coming for some reason. I try to keep my voice chirpy, but it comes out sort of flat, sort of underhand. 'I'm away out.' And while I'm drawing the door off the **snib**, gently so as not to wake Irene up, Mammy appears suddenly, her face hanging, at the top of the lobby.

'Where are you away to already?'

'Joe's.' I'm stalling. Then she sighs. I can hear it all the way down the lobby.

'Will you be home for your tea?'

There's a funny edge about her voice. She's really upset about something and I can see it all over her face. But I don't know what she wants me to say.

'You tell me nothing. Will you not even be in for your tea?' Her breathing is funny as well.

There's me at the other end of the lobby, feeling guilty, but I haven't a clue what I've done and I don't know how to make it better. I know she sometimes resents me going out all the time, but she just moans if I stay in. So I squirm for a minute and grab the compromise: 'Aye, okay. Okay, I'll be in for my tea,' and I shut the door fast, desperate to get out in the fresh

---

snib: latch

air. I stand for a minute at the door, just breathing it in with my eyes shut.

Joe's still in his bed when I get to his place. I've to wake him up by **chapping** on the window and pulling faces in at him. One of the cats gets up on the window-sill when it sees me and we both climb in the window together, me laughing and calling Joe a lazy so-and-so and the cat rubbing itself like crazy off his ankles and purring for something to eat; Joe smiling away in the middle of it.

Joe's great; really good-natured. I don't think I've ever seen him lose his temper. Every other day I get him up out of bed and he just smiles and gets me something to drink and we have breakfast together. I think the house has something to do with it. He lives in this big house on the shore front and more or less on his own. His mother (a widow, like mine) stays out a lot, sometimes for days on end; and his brother's so quiet you wouldn't even know he was there half the time – he sort of tiptoes about the place. Or goes out, too. So Joe gets the run of the place; him and the three cats and the rabbit. Oh – and the tropical fish. He's been buying these tropical fish recently and he can sit and stare at them for hours. Some nights we get in a takeaway and just sit in his room watching the fish and eating the food and talking till we fall asleep. And even then, it's still me wakes him up in the morning.

Anyway, Joe's in the house by himself this morning. He fixes some grub for us and the cats, then we're out for a walk. Not that we do much or go very far: just

---

chapping: knocking

down the rocks to look for anemones, beachcomb along the sand till we get cold. We go up the town after that and buy two cups of coffee at the Melbourne to warm our hands off them and get hysterical at the man telling us it's time we were married. He says that every time we go in there. We keep telling him we're not going out or anything, just friends, and it doesn't make any difference. I don't know whether he doesn't believe us or whether it's just a good joke for him. Joe's mother certainly doesn't think it's a joke. She's always getting on about me seeing him all the time, and wasn't it time I got myself a *proper boyfriend* and I should stop staying overnight because I'd *get a name about myself*. Joe gets really grim when she does that. It's as if they don't want us to be friends or something. Or probably don't believe that's all there is to it. Dirty minds.

We stay in there a long time, **blethering**. The man gives us another cup of coffee for nothing because we stay in so long and asks us what on earth we find to talk about. I couldn't tell him. It's everything and nothing. We just sort of spark each other off and we never seem to get bored with each other. This time, we're talking about the look on my mother's face this morning, but we shut up when the man comes over. Joe gets back to it after the coffee arrives, speaking and stirring with the spoon. 'She's likely just fed up,' he says. 'Just wanting you to talk to for a change. Maybe she's lonely.'

I say nothing.

'It's just not in her to ask you to stay in, either. She wants you to want to stay in.'

---

blethering: talking

Now I know he's right. But I also know, and he does too, that it isn't in *me* to stay in while Irene's there. Holidays are murder.

We've finished the second cups now and Joe's up to buy a quarter of sweeties. We walk from one end of Dockhead Street to the other eating them, then back up again. Most of the shops are still closed for the New Year but it doesn't matter; we've hardly any money anyway. We're just looking. And we keep blethering the whole time. We end up back at his place with more warm coffee, staring out at the waterfront from the bay window and still talking and stroking the cats. I'm really mellow by this time, with the water and the brightness of the day and the feel of the cats' fur under our hands – full of that nice, relaxed sort of tiredness you get after a long walk. I'm happy. Then I look at my watch. My face is sliding while I'm standing up.

'I said I'd go back for my tea. I better shift.'

But he knows I'm not wanting to and he knows fine why. I keep looking out the window for a wee bit, holding on to it before I have to let go.

'I'll be away then.'

And all the time he knows perfectly well I'm dreading it, and the good time we were having isn't making it any easier. It's making it worse. I'm hoping he's going to offer to walk me back or something, then suddenly his face lights up.

'I'll come round and be your first foot! Bet that would cheer your mother up. We'll buy a bottle of that stuff she likes, take some shortbread, do the thing right . . .' And he's off into the kitchen hunting up money and biscuit tins. I'm pretty taken with the idea. Mammy likes Joe, he can make a difference to her. And the daftness of the first foot thing will make us all laugh. We'll have a present for her as well: she'll say we shouldn't have but she'll be pleased all the same. It gets better and better as I think about it.

Outside, we count up the rest of Joe's Christmas money and the **dregs** of my cash – enough for a half bottle of advocaat and a wee jar of cocktail cherries, for a touch of celebration. But it takes us ages to find some place that'll sell us the drink. Bloody hell, I think, it's only advocaat. Mammy isn't too happy with drink in the house, but she does like this stuff – it doesn't count. Especially when you mix it up with lemonade. They call it a snowball and you can even give it to **weans**, for goodness sake. We were giggling all the way up the road about it. I'm all warm and excited by this time, really happy inside and looking forward to springing the surprise. Me and my best friend; taking our good time and bringing it home in triumph for my mammy to share. She's always saying life doesn't give her many laughs, but when it does, she knows how to enjoy them. She's great fun when she's in the mood. And here's me bringing luck to the house with the first foot and the bottle. O aye, I'm looking forward to it.

The sight of the front door calms me down a bit, though. Irene, I think. She's been murder for the past two days and I can't afford to give her any excuse. She doesn't like me bringing folk in the house – and she doesn't like Joe. Still, no problem. We can go in the kitchenette and wait, then Mammy will come through

---

dregs: last bits
weans: babies, small children

to see what's keeping me. Fine, we can wait in there and have the drinks ready for her coming through.

I push open the door gently, shouting, 'It's me,' at the closed living-room and the two of us sneak into the kitchenette. I start looking for the glasses and Joe gets the tissue paper off the wee bottle. He's still laughing when she comes through. She just stands there in the door with her face deadly and me with my smile frozen and stuck in place.

'Where the hell have you been?'

And I just stand rooted. I'm getting dizzy.

'Where the hell were you? You said you'd be home for your tea. I had it ready for you ages ago. It's over there, cold and dry as dust. And you'll bloody well eat it if it chokes ye. Good money wasted.'

Her face is really bitter. She's noticed Joe and flinches a bit with being so angry in front of him, but that doesn't stop it. And the violence of it knocks the stuffing out of me and everything I wanted to say.

Joe fumbles in: 'She's been at my place, Mrs Galloway, we've been –'

But she's too mad to listen. She's shouting: 'Well take her back there then. On ye go. Never want to be in here anyway; quick as ye can get out in the mornings. On ye go. Get out of my sight. Away with your friends: let them feed ye.' Her whole body is trembling.

I'm trapped with my own speechlessness. I'm wanting to yell, to make her see. I want her to notice the bottle we've brought. And she does see it, but only with her eyes. It still doesn't mean anything to her – just a bottle on the table and a jar of daft cherries. I want her to really see it, recognise it for what I mean it to be – some kind of a token and some sort of prayer it's impossible to speak out loud in this damned house. I want her to see all that at once and stop, take it and pour it out and drink hopefully to the New Year; to accept it. Accept *me*. It's not just a bloody drink I've brought her – I'm trying to tell her I love her. But I know she's too blind and too angry. And I know who's done the blinding. Irene.

I want to scream, but I know I won't. I never do. Instead, I just burn with guilt, shame and self-disgust.

I'd been stupid. I should have known what my sister could do when my back was turned. Then her voice floats in, sickly sweet, from the living-room. 'Don't upset yourself with her, Mammy. Just come away through. Leave her with her "friend".' And my mother just turns her heel and goes.

Me and Joe just stand in the kitchenette. He doesn't speak, he's waiting, afraid for what I might do. Then I feel the tears starting down my face and I run to hide in the bedroom, just stand and stare at the frozen washing still on the line outside. My jaw hurts with biting it down: *Mammy, don't listen to her, help me to find the words for once*. But it goes on hurting and I know I won't say it. I know I won't ever say it.

Staring, cursing our weakness, I make up my mind. *Let her win*.

I start gathering my things together.

Urban myths: The Choking Alsatian *and* The Vanishing Hitchhiker

These very short stories, from America and England, are from the oral tradition and from popular rather than literary culture. They have been passed on from one teller to another, and tellers will often add their own descriptions to make them more spooky and gripping. These urban myths are not necessarily true, but are the kind of tales that people believe because they are told to them by a friend or relative.

As you read, *try to identify the differences between them. Why is* The Choking Alsatian *more believable and eerie than* The Vanishing Hitchhiker?

Megan had always wanted a dog – preferably a big, ferocious dog that would make her feel safe at night. Her boyfriend put all sorts of arguments against it, saying that the house was too small, or that they hadn't time to spend with it. But none of them were convincing, and Megan had long since been certain of what was, in fact, the truth – that Alex simply disliked dogs. Still, it wasn't worth arguing over a pet – there were so many other things to argue about anyway . . .

But after one argument too many, Megan finally summoned the courage to leave Alex. Being a woman who didn't like to do things by halves, she moved away as far as she could – to Australia. Settling down in her house in Queensland, surveying the empty land all around her which extended about as far as the whole of the dreary city centre where she used to live, it was with the feeling almost of a naughty child that Megan realised she finally had a decent excuse to get herself a guard dog. She had wanted one ever since she could remember, but only now could she hear her father's voice in her head, telling her that her new home was in an unfriendly and dangerous place, and that it was as well to be cautious.

After several weeks, however, Megan had to admit that her father was wrong. The neighbours (if you could call them neighbours, as the nearest lived some eight miles away) had been almost disappointingly friendly. Not only this, but the most dangerous excursion that Bruno – her beautiful, strong Alsatian – ever had to make was crossing the road on his softly padded way to the vet for his vaccinations. Megan had to admire the way the vet calmly handled the dog who could have snapped his arm off at the wrist with one false move.

One day, coming back from work, Megan was disappointed and a little worried to find that Bruno had not bounded up to greet her as he *always* did. Running upstairs, calling for him, she noticed – or thought she noticed – a tiny movement in the corner of her living room, behind the sofa. But that was surely nerves . . . and anyway, here was Bruno, after all. He was clearly not well, though, and Megan reproached herself for the disloyal thoughts she had allowed to cross her mind; there was no way, with that cough, that Bruno could have run to greet her. He did not seem ill in any other way, however; his coat was shiny, his eyes bright. Megan bent down and, back straining, hoisted him up. She carried him off to the car, and went back into the house to call the vet. Again, she felt the tiniest shift of air in the living room, but, looking around, there was nothing abnormal. The vet's familiar voice calmed her, and having briefly explained the situation, she drove Bruno into Cairns, the nearest town, to drop him off.

Having dropped Bruno off at the surgery and collected some groceries in town, Megan made her way home. It was a fairly long drive, and she was pleased when she finally pulled up outside her house. As she walked up the drive, she could hear the phone ringing inside. She almost checked herself as she broke into a run – after all, whoever was ringing was scarcely worth breaking a sweat over – but then habit took over and she caught the phone before it rang off.

'Hello?' she said, testily – she felt a bit uneasy. It was okay though, it was only the vet . . .

'Megan, I've found out what's wrong with your dog. You have to come here straight away. Just walk out of the door and right back into your car!' She had never heard him this anxious before, and for the life of her she could not work out why. She slumped a little, worried now.

'Is it something awful? Is he dying?' Suddenly, without warning, she began to cry, rocking backwards and forwards. It was not fair that she had got her dog at last, only to have him taken away from her after barely six months. Irrationally, she felt it was some long-distance trick of Alex's, still determined as he was to spoil her happiness. With a start, she realised that the vet was still talking to her.

'Please, Megan!' He was shouting now. 'It's nothing to do with the dog – at least, it is, but . . . anyway, that doesn't matter! Just promise me you'll get the hell out of there. If I hear you speak again, instead of running to your car, I'm going to get angry. Okay? Okay?'

Megan was silent for a moment. The vet was about to ring off, but then, prompted by Megan's rapid, shallow breaths, he spoke once more.

'Megan, listen very carefully. The reason Bruno was choking was that he had a hand stuck in his throat! A human hand, do you understand? There's somebody in the house Megan! Get out of there!'

Suddenly, the line went dead.

The Vanishing Hitchhiker

A friend of a friend was cruising down the A1 to London when he passed a young lady standing by the side of the road. He pulled up and asked her if she needed a lift. Without speaking, she got into the car. He was quite attracted to her, so he tried to get her talking, but she just wouldn't say anything, not even where she was getting off. Instead, at the junction, she pointed. Then at her road, and then at her house, where she got out of the car. He drove off in a huff.

A couple of days later, he was looking for something in the car when he came across a woman's coat. Knowing it must be the hitchhiker's he retraced his route to return the coat to her. So he knocked on the door and an older lady opened it. He held out the coat and explained that he wanted to return it to the young woman. The woman burst into tears. 'Yes, it was my daughter's,' she spluttered, 'but she was killed on the A1 five years ago.'

The Sniper

Liam O'Flaherty

This is an exciting, violent story, full of suspense, about a lone gunman. Once he is injured, he uses wily tactics to try to survive. The writer was born in 1896 and is a famous figure in Irish literature. He was a soldier in World War One and was involved in revolutionary activities in Ireland. This story is set in the Irish Civil War.

As you read, *notice how this skilled writer describes only a few events but in great detail. This is something that younger writers often find difficult, as they tend to write about many events and actions without much description. Notice how he manages to maintain our interest throughout the story. Can you spot the methods he uses to do this?*

The long June twilight faded into night. Dublin lay enveloped in darkness but for the dim light of the moon that shone through fleecy clouds, casting a pale light as of approaching dawn over the streets and the dark waters of the Liffey. Around the **beleaguered** Four Courts the heavy guns roared. Here and there through the city, machine guns and rifles broke the silence of the night, **spasmodically**, like dogs barking on lone farms. Republicans and Free Staters were waging civil war.

---

beleaguered: under great pressure
spasmodically: jerkily

On a rooftop near O'Connell Bridge, a Republican **sniper** lay watching. Beside him lay his rifle and over his shoulders was slung a pair of field glasses. His face was the face of a student, thin and **ascetic**, but his eyes had the cold gleam of the **fanatic**. They were deep and thoughtful, the eyes of a man who is used to looking at death.

He was eating a sandwich hungrily. He had eaten nothing since morning. He had been too excited to eat. He finished the sandwich, and, taking a flask of whiskey from his pocket, he took a short **draught**. Then he returned the flask to his pocket. He paused for a moment, considering whether he should risk a smoke. It was dangerous. The flash might be seen in the darkness, and there were enemies watching. He decided to take the risk.

Placing a cigarette between his lips, he struck a match, inhaled the smoke hurriedly and put out the light. Almost immediately, a bullet flattened itself against the **parapet** of the roof. The sniper took another whiff and put out the cigarette. Then he swore softly and crawled away to the left.

Cautiously he raised himself and peered over the parapet. There was a flash and a bullet whizzed over his head. He dropped immediately. He had seen the flash. It came from the opposite side of the street.

---

sniper: gunman who picks people off from distant cover
ascetic: disciplined
fanatic: religious maniac
draught: swallow
parapet: low wall around a flat roof

He rolled over the roof to a chimney stack in the rear, and slowly drew himself up behind it, until his eyes were level with the top of the parapet. There was nothing to be seen – just the dim outline of the opposite housetop against the blue sky. His enemy was under cover.

Just then an armoured car came across the bridge and advanced slowly up the street. It stopped on the opposite side of the street, fifty yards ahead. The sniper could hear the dull panting of the motor. His heart beat faster. It was an enemy car. He wanted to fire, but he knew it was useless. His bullets would never pierce the steel that covered the grey monster.

Then round the corner of a side street came an old woman, her head covered by a tattered shawl. She began to talk to the man in the turret of the car. She was pointing to the roof where the sniper lay. An informer.

The turret opened. A man's head and shoulders appeared, looking toward the sniper. The sniper raised his rifle and fired. The head fell heavily on the turret wall. The woman darted toward the side street. The sniper fired again. The woman whirled round and fell with a shriek into the gutter.

Suddenly from the opposite roof a shot rang out and the sniper dropped his rifle with a curse. The rifle clattered to the roof. The sniper thought the noise would wake the dead. He stooped to pick the rifle up. He couldn't lift it. His forearm was dead. 'I'm hit,' he muttered.

Dropping flat onto the roof, he crawled back to the parapet. With his left hand he felt the injured right forearm. The blood was oozing through the sleeve of his coat. There was no pain – just a deadened sensation, as if the arm had been cut off.

Quickly he drew his knife from his pocket, opened it on the breastwork of the parapet, and ripped open the sleeve. There was a small hole where the bullet had entered. On the other side there was no hole. The bullet had lodged in the bone. It must have fractured it. He bent the arm below the wound. The arm bent back easily. He ground his teeth to overcome the pain.

Then taking out his field dressing, he ripped open the packet with his knife. He broke the neck of the iodine bottle and let the bitter fluid drip into the wound. A **paroxysm** of pain swept through him. He placed the cotton wadding over the wound and wrapped the dressing over it. He tied the ends with his teeth.

Then he lay still against the parapet, and, closing his eyes, he made an effort of will to overcome the pain.

In the street beneath all was still. The armoured car had retired speedily over the bridge, with the machine gunner's head hanging lifeless over the turret. The woman's corpse lay still in the gutter.

The sniper lay still for a long time nursing his wounded arm and planning escape. Morning must not find him wounded on the roof. The enemy on the opposite roof covered his escape. He must kill that enemy and he could not use his rifle. He had only a revolver to do it. Then he thought of a plan.

Taking off his cap, he placed it over the muzzle of his rifle. Then he pushed the rifle slowly upward over the parapet, until the cap was visible from the opposite side of the street. Almost immediately there was a **report**, and a bullet pierced the centre of the cap. The

paroxysm: spasm
report: loud bang

sniper slanted the rifle forward. The cap clipped down into the street. Then catching the rifle in the middle, the sniper dropped his left hand over the roof and let it hang, lifelessly. After a few moments he let the rifle drop to the street. Then he sank to the roof, dragging his hand with him.

Crawling quickly to his feet, he peered up at the corner of the roof. His **ruse** had succeeded. The other sniper, seeing the cap and rifle fall, thought that he had killed his man. He was now standing before a row of chimney pots, looking across, with his head clearly silhouetted against the western sky.

The Republican sniper smiled and lifted his revolver above the edge of the parapet. The distance was about

---

ruse: trick

fifty yards – a hard shot in the dim light, and his right arm was paining him like a thousand devils. He took a steady aim. His hand trembled with eagerness. Pressing his lips together, he took a deep breath through his nostrils and fired. He was almost deafened with the report and his arm shook with the recoil.

Then when the smoke cleared, he peered across and uttered a cry of joy. His enemy had been hit. He was reeling over the parapet in his death agony. He struggled to keep his feet, but he was slowly falling forward as if in a dream. The rifle fell from his grasp, hit the parapet, fell over, bounced off the pole of a barber's shop beneath and then clattered on the pavement.

Then the dying man on the roof crumpled up and fell forward. The body turned over and over in space and hit the ground with a dull thud. Then it lay still.

The sniper looked at his enemy falling and he shuddered. The lust of battle died in him. He became bitten by **remorse**. The sweat stood out in beads on his forehead. Weakened by his wound and the long summer day of fasting and watching on the roof, he revolted from the sight of the shattered mass of his dead enemy. His teeth chattered, he began to gibber to himself, cursing the war, cursing himself, cursing everybody.

He looked at the smoking revolver in his hand, and with an oath he hurled it to the roof at his feet. The revolver went off with a **concussion** and the bullet whizzed past the sniper's head. He was frightened back to his senses by the shock. His nerves steadied. The cloud of fear scattered from his mind and he laughed.

remorse: sorrow and regret
concussion: shock

Taking the whiskey flask from his pocket, he emptied it at a draught. He felt reckless under the influence of the spirit. He decided to leave the roof now and look for his company commander, to report. Everywhere around was quiet. There was not much danger in going through the streets. He picked up his revolver and put it in his pocket. Then he crawled down through the skylight to the house underneath.

When the sniper reached the laneway on the street level, he felt a sudden curiosity as to the identity of the enemy sniper whom he had killed. He decided that he was a good shot, whoever he was. He wondered did he know him. Perhaps he had been in his own company before the split in the army. He decided to risk going over to have a look at him. He peered around the corner into O'Connell Street. In the upper part of the street there was heavy firing, but around here all was quiet.

The sniper darted across the street. A machine gun tore up the ground around him with a hail of bullets, but he escaped. He threw himself face downward beside the corpse. The machine gun stopped.

Then the sniper turned over the dead body and looked into his brother's face.

The Friendship

Mildred D. Taylor

Mildred D. Taylor was born in Mississippi in the American South. This area of America has a history of black slavery and tension between black and white people. Although her family moved north, when they visited the South she was shocked by the violence of the racism there, but also moved by the love and pride she found in her family and the black community. This prize-winning story is based on a true story the writer heard from her father.

As you read, *notice how Mildred D. Taylor creates such different and believable characters. Think carefully about the character of Jeremy in this story, and why he is important to the plot.*

'Now don't y'all go touchin' nothin',' Stacey warned as we stepped onto the porch of the Wallace store. Christopher-John, Little Man, and I readily agreed to that. After all, we weren't even supposed to be up here. 'And Cassie,' he added, 'don't you say nothin'.'

'Now, boy, what I'm gonna say?' I cried, indignant that he should single me out.

'Just mind my words, hear? Now come on.' Stacey started for the door, then stepped back as Jeremy Simms, a blond sad-eyed boy, came out. Looking out from under the big straw hat he was wearing, he glanced somewhat shyly at us, then gave a nod. We took a moment and nodded back. At first I thought Jeremy was going to say something. He looked as if he wanted to, but then he walked on past and went slowly down the steps. We all watched him. He got as far as the corner of the porch and looked back. The boys and I turned and went into the store.

Once inside we stood in the entrance a moment, somewhat hesitant now about being here. At the back counter, two of the storekeepers, Thurston and Dewberry Wallace, were stocking shelves. They glanced over, then paid us no further attention. I didn't much like them. Mama and Papa didn't much like them either. They didn't much like any of the Wallaces and that included Dewberry and Thurston's brother, Kaleb, and their father, John. They said the Wallaces didn't treat our folks right and it was best to stay clear of them. Because of that they didn't come up to this store to shop and we weren't supposed to be coming up here either.

We all knew that. But today as we had walked the red road towards home, Aunt Callie Jackson, who wasn't really our aunt but whom everybody called that because she was so old, had **hollered** to us from her front porch and said she had the headache bad. She said her nephew Joe was gone off somewhere and she had nobody to send to the store for head medicine. We couldn't say no to her, not to Aunt Callie. So despite Mama's and Papa's warnings about this Wallace place, we had taken it upon ourselves to come anyway. Stacey had said they would understand and after a moment's thought had added that if they didn't he would take the blame and that had settled it. After all, he was twelve with three years on me, so I made no

---

hollered: called

objection about the thing. Christopher-John and Little Man, younger still, nodded agreement and that was that.

'Now mind what I said,' Stacey warned us again, then headed for the back counter and the Wallaces. Christopher-John, Little Man, and I remained by the front door looking the store over; it was our first time in the place. The store was small, not nearly as large as it had looked from the outside peeping in. Farm supplies and household and food goods were sparsely displayed on the shelves and counters and the floor space too, while on the walls were plastered posters of a man called **Roosevelt**. In the centre of the store was a pot-bellied stove, and near it a table and some chairs. But nobody was sitting there. In fact, there were no other customers in the store.

Our eyes roamed over it all with little interest; then we spotted the three large jars of candy on one of the counters. One was filled with lemon drops, another with liquorice, and a third with candy canes. Christopher-John, who was seven, round, and had himself a mighty sweet tooth, glanced around at Little Man and me, grinning. Then he walked over to the candy jars for a closer look. There he stood staring at them with a hungry longing even though he knew good and well there would be no candy for him this day. There never was for any of us except at Christmas-time. Little Man started to follow him, but then something else caught his eye. Something gleaming and shining. Belt buckles and lockets, cuff-links, and tie-clips in a glass case. As soon as Little Man saw them,

---

Roosevelt: President of the USA 1932–44

he forgot about the jars of candy and strutted right over. Little Man loved shiny new things.

Not interested in drooling over candy I knew I couldn't have, or shiny new things either, I went on to the back and stood with Stacey. Since the Wallaces were taking their own good time about serving us, I busied myself studying a brand-new 1933 catalogue that lay open on the counter. Finally, Dewberry asked what we wanted. Stacey was about to tell him, but before he could, Dewberry's eyes suddenly widened and he slapped the rag he was holding against the counter and hollered, 'Get them filthy hands off-a-there!'

Stacey and I turned to see who he was yelling at. So did Christopher-John. Then we saw Little Man. Excited by the lure of all those shiny new things, Little Man had forgotten Stacey's warning. Standing on tiptoe, he was bracing himself with both hands against the top of the glass counter for a better look inside. Now he glanced around. He found Dewberry's eyes on him and snatched his hands away. He hid them behind his back.

Dewberry, a full-grown man, stared down at Little Man. Little Man, only six, looked up. 'Now I'm gonna hafta clean that glass again,' snapped Dewberry, 'seeing you done put them dirty hands-a yours all over it!'

'My hands ain't dirty,' Little Man calmly informed him. He seemed happy that he could set Dewberry's mind to rest if that was all that was bothering him. Little Man pulled his hands from behind his back and inspected them. He turned his hands inward. He turned them outward. Then he held them up for Dewberry to see. 'They clean!' he said. 'They ain't dirty! They clean!'

Dewberry came from around the corner. 'Boy, you disputin' my word? Just look at ya! Skin's black as dirt. Could put seeds on ya and have 'em growin' in no time!'

Thurston Wallace laughed and tossed his brother an axe from one of the shelves. 'Best chop them hands off, Dew, they that filthy!'

Little Man's eyes widened at the sight of the axe. He slapped his hands behind himself again and backed away. Stacey hurried over and put an arm around him. Keeping eyes on the Wallaces, he brought Little Man back to stand with us. Thurston and Dewberry laughed.

We got Aunt Callie's head medicine and hurried out. As we reached the steps we ran into Mr Tom Bee carrying a fishing pole and two strings of fish. Mr Tom Bee was an elderly, toothless man who had a bit of **sharecropping** land over on the Granger Plantation. But Mr Tom Bee didn't do much farming these days. Instead he spent most of his days fishing. Mr Tom Bee loved to fish. 'Well now,' he said, coming up the steps, 'where y'all younguns headed to?'

Stacey nodded towards the crossroads. 'Over to Aunt Callie's, then on home.'

'Y'all hold on up a minute, I walk with ya. Got a mess-a fish for Aunt Callie. Jus' wants to drop off this here other string and get me some more-a my sardines. I loves fishin' cat, but I keeps me a taste for sardines!' he laughed.

Stacey watched him go into the store, then looked back to the road. There wasn't much to see. There was

---

sharecropping: small farming

a lone **gas** pump in front of the store. There were two red roads that crossed each other, and a dark forest that loomed on the other three corners of the crossroads. That was all, yet Stacey was staring out intensely as if there were more to see. A troubled look was on his face and anger was in his eyes.

'You figure we best head on home?' I asked.

'Reckon we can wait, Mr Tom Bee don't take too long,' he said, then leaned moodily back against the post. I knew his moods and I knew this one had nothing to do with Mr Tom Bee. So I let him be and sat down on the steps in the shade of the porch trying to escape some of the heat. It was miserably hot. But then it most days was in a Mississippi summer. Christopher-John sat down too, but not Little Man. He remained by the open doors staring into the store. Christopher-John noticed him there and immediately hopped back up again. Always sympathising with other folks' feelings, he went over to Little Man and tried to comfort him. 'Don'tcha worry now, Man,' he said, patting his shoulder. 'Don'tcha worry! We knows you ain't dirty!'

'That ain't what they said!' shrieked Little Man, his voice revealing the hurt he felt. Little Man took great pride in being clean.

Stacey turned to them. 'Man, forget about what they said. You can't pay them no mind.'

'But, St-Stacey! They said they could plant seeds on me!' he cried indignantly.

I looked back at him. 'Ah, shoot, boy! You know they can't do no such-a thing!'

---

gas: petrol

Sceptically Little Man looked to Stacey for **affirmation**.

Stacey nodded. 'They can do plenty all right, but they can't do nothin' like that.'

'But – but, Stacey, th-they s-said they was g-gonna c-cut off my hands. They done s-said they gonna do that c-cause they . . . they dirty!'

Stacey said nothing for a moment, then pulled from the post and went over to him. 'They was jus' teasin' you, Man,' he said softly, 'that's all. They was jus' teasin'. Their way of funnin'.'

'Wasn't nothin' 'bout it funny to me,' I remarked, feeling Little Man's hurt.

Stacey's eyes met mine and I knew he was feeling the same. He brought Little Man back to the steps and the two of them sat down. Little Man, seemingly comforted with Stacey beside him, was silent now. But after a few moments he did a strange thing. He reached down and placed his hand flat to the dirt. He looked at his hand, looked at the dirt, then drew back again. Without a word, he folded his hands tightly together and held them very still in his lap.

I looked at the ground, then at him. 'Now what was all that about?'

Little Man looked at me, his eyes deeply troubled. And once again, Stacey said, 'Forget it, Man, forget it.'

Little Man said nothing, but I could tell he wasn't forgetting anything. I stared down at the dirt. I wasn't forgetting either.

''Ey, y'all.'

Sceptically: with disbelief
affirmation: agreement

We turned. Jeremy Simms was standing at the corner of the porch.

'Boy, I thought you was gone!' I said.

Stacey nudged me to be quiet, but didn't say anything to Jeremy himself. Jeremy bit at his lip, his face reddening. Rubbing one bare foot against the other, he pushed his hands deep into his overall pockets. 'C-come up here to wait on my pa and R.W. and Melvin,' he explained. 'Got a load to pick up. Been waiting a good while now.'

Stacey nodded. There wasn't anything to say to that. Jeremy seemed to understand there was nothing to say. A fly buzzed near his face. He brushed it away, looked out at the crossroads, then sat down at the end of the porch and leaned against a post facing us. He pulled one leg up towards his chest and left the other leg dangling over the side of the porch. He glanced at us, looked out at the crossroads, then back at us again. 'Y'all . . . y'all been doin' a lotta fishin' here lately?'

Stacey glanced over. 'Fish when we can.'

'Over on the Rosa Lee?'

Stacey nodded his answer.

'I fish over there sometimes . . .'

'Most folks do . . .' said Stacey.

Jeremy was silent a moment as if thinking on what he should say next. 'Y'all . . . y'all spect to be goin' fishin' again anyways soon?'

Stacey shook his head. 'Cotton time's here. Got too much work to do now for much fishin'.'

'Yeah, me too I reckon . . .'

Jeremy looked away once more and was quiet once more. I watched him, trying to figure him out. The boy was a mighty puzzlement to me, the way he was always talking friendly to us. I didn't understand it. He was white.

Stacey saw me staring and shook his head, letting me know I shouldn't be doing it. So I stopped. After that we all just sat there in the muggy midday heat listening to the sounds of bees and flies and cawing blackbirds and kept our silence. Then we heard voices rising inside the store and turned to look. Mr Tom Bee, the string of fish and the fishing pole still in his hand, was standing before the counter listening to Dewberry.

'Now look here, old uncle,' said Dewberry, 'I told you three times my daddy's busy! You tell me what you want or get on outa here. I ain't got all day to fool with you.'

Mr Tom Bee was a slightly built man, and that along with his age made him look somewhat **frail**, and especially so as he faced the much younger Dewberry. But that look of frailty didn't keep him from speaking his mind. There was a sharp-edged stubbornness to Mr Tom Bee. His eyes ran over both Dewberry and Thurston and he snapped: 'Give me some-a them sardines! Needs me four cans!'

Dewberry leaned across the counter. 'You already got plenty-a **charges**, Tom. You don't need no sardines. Ya stinkin' of fish as it is.'

I nudged Stacey. 'Now how he know what Mr Tom Bee need?'

Stacey told me to hush.

'Well, shoot! Mr Tom Bee been grown more years than 'bout anybody 'round here! He oughta know what he need!'

---

frail: weak
charges: purchases on credit

'Cassie, I said hush!' Stacey glanced back towards the store as if afraid somebody inside might have heard. Then he glanced over at Jeremy, who bit his lower lip and looked away again as if he had heard nothing at all.

Saying nothing else, Stacey looked back at the crossroads. I cut my eyes at him, then sighed. I was tired of always having to watch my mouth whenever white folks were around. Wishing Mr Tom Bee would get his stuff and come on, I got up and crossed the porch to the doorway. It was then I saw that Christopher-John had eased back inside and was again staring up at the candy jars. I started to tell Stacey that Christopher-John was in the store, then realised Mr Tom Bee had noticed him too. Seeing Christopher-John standing there, Mr Tom Bee pointed to the candy and said to Dewberry, 'An' you can jus' give me some-a them candy canes there too.'

'Don't need no candy canes neither, Tom,' decided Dewberry. 'Got no teeth to chew 'em with.'

Mr Tom Bee stood his ground. 'Y'all can't get them sardines and that candy for me, y'all go get y'alls daddy and let him get it! Where John anyway?' he demanded. 'He give me what I ask for, you sorry boys won't!'

Suddenly the store went quiet. I could feel something was wrong. Stacey got up. I looked at him. We both knew this name business was a touchy thing. I didn't really understand why, but it was. White folks took it seriously. Mighty seriously. They took it seriously to call every grown black person straight out by their first name without placing a 'mister' or a 'missus' or a 'miss' anywhere. White folks, young and old, called Mama and Papa straight out by their first names. They called Big Ma by her first name or they sometimes called her

aunty because she was in her sixties now and that was
their way of showing her age some respect, though Big
Ma said she didn't need that kind of respect. She
wasn't *their* aunty. They took seriously too the way we
addressed them. All the white grown folks I knew
expected to be addressed proper with that 'mister' and
'missus' sounding loud ahead of their names. No,
I didn't understand it. But I understood enough to
know Mr Tom Bee could be in trouble standing up in
this store calling Dewberry and Thurston's father John
straight out.

Jeremy glanced from the store to us, watching, his
lips pressed tight. I could tell he understood the
seriousness of names too. Stacey moved towards me. It
was then he saw Christopher-John inside the store. He
bit his lip nervously, as if trying to decide if he should
bring attention to Christopher-John by going in to get
him. I think the quiet made him wait.

Dewberry pointed a warning finger at Mr Tom Bee.
'Old nigger,' he said, 'don't you never in this life speak
to me that way again. And don't you never stand up
there with yo' black face and speak of my daddy or any
other white man without the proper respect. You might
be of a forgetful mind at yo' age, but you forgettin' the
wrong thing when you forgettin' who you are. A nigger,
nothin' but a nigger. You may be old, Tom, but you ain't
too old to teach and you ain't too old to whip!'

My breath caught and I shivered. It was such a little
thing, I figured, this thing about a name. I just couldn't
understand it. I just couldn't understand it at all.

The back door to the store slammed and a man
appeared in the doorway. He was average-built and
looked to be somewhere in his fifties. The man was

John Wallace, Dewberry and Thurston's father. He looked at Mr Tom Bee, then motioned to his sons. 'I take care-a this,' he said.

Mr Tom Bee grinned. 'Well, howdy there, John!' he exclaimed. 'Glad ya finally done brought yourself on in here! These here boys-a yours ain't been none too friendly.'

John Wallace looked solemnly at Mr Tom Bee. 'What ya want, Tom?'

'Wants me my sardines and some candy there, John.'

Dewberry slammed his fist hard upon the counter. 'Daddy! How come you to let this old nigger disrespect ya this here way? Just lettin' him stand there and talk to you like he was a white man! He need teachin', Daddy! He need teachin'!'

'Dew's right,' said Thurston. 'Them old **britches** done stretched way too big!'

John Wallace wheeled around and fixed hard, unrelenting eyes on his sons. 'Y'all hush up and get on to ya business! There's stackin' to be done out back!'

'But, Daddy –'

'I said get!'

For a moment Dewberry and Thurston didn't move. The heat seemed more stifling. The quiet more quiet. John Wallace kept eyes on his sons. Dewberry and Thurston left the store.

As the back door closed behind them Stacey went in and got Christopher-John. Mr John Wallace took note of him, took note of all of us, and as Stacey and Christopher-John came out he came behind and closed the doors. But he forgot the open windows. He turned

britches: trousers

back to Mr Tom Bee. 'Now, Tom,' he said, 'I done told you before 'bout calling me by my Christian name, it ain't jus' the two of us. It ain't seemly, you here a nigger and me a white man. Now you ain't used to do it. Some folks say it's yo' old age. Say your age is making you forget 'bout way things is. But I say it ain't your age, it's your **orneriness**.'

Mr Tom Bee squared his shoulders. 'An' I done tole you, it ain't seemly t' me to be callin' no white man mister when I done saved his **sorry hide** when he wasn't hardly no older'n them younguns standin' out yonder! You owes me, John. Ya knows ya owes me too.'

John Wallace walked back to the counter. 'Ain't necessarily what I'm wanting, but what's gotta be. You just can't keep going 'round calling me by my first name no more. Folks been taking note. Makes me look bad. Even my boys been questionin' me on why I lets ya do it.'

'Then tell 'em, doggonit!'

'I'm losin' face, Tom.'

'Now, what you think I care 'bout your face, boy? I done saved your hide more'n one time and I gots me a right t'call you whatsoever I pleases t'call you whensoever I be talkin' t' ya!'

John Wallace sucked in his breath. 'Naw, Tom, not no more.'

Mr Tom Bee sucked in his breath too. 'You figure the years done made you forget how come you alive an' still breathin'?'

---

orneriness: stubbornness
sorry hide: life

'Figure the years done give me sense 'bout this thing.'

'Well, you live long 'nough, maybe the next years gonna give you the sense 'nough t' be grateful. Now put these here sardines on my charges.' He glanced over at the candy jars. 'An' give me two pennies' worth-a them there candy sticks while's you at it.'

Mr Tom Bee stood quietly waiting as if expecting his order to be obeyed, and to our surprise Mr John Wallace did obey. He reached into the candy jar, pulled out a fistful of candy canes, and handed them to him. Mr Tom Bee took the candy canes and gave John Wallace a nod. Mr John Wallace put both hands flat on the counter.

'Tom, mind what I say now. My patience done worn thin 'bout 'mindin' you 'bout what's proper. Next time you come in here, you make sure you address me right, you hear?'

Mr Tom Bee cackled a laugh and slapped one string of fish on the counter. 'These here for you, John. Knows how much you like catfish so these here for you!' Then, still chuckling, he picked up his cans of sardines and stuffed them into his pockets, turned his back on John Wallace, and left the store.

As soon as Mr Tom Bee was outside, he looked down at Christopher-John and said, 'How'd y'all younguns like a little bit-a candy?'

'Like it just fine, Mr Tom Bee!' spoke up Christopher-John.

Mr Tom Bee laughed and handed him a stick, then presented one each to Stacey, Little Man, and me. Stacey, Christopher-John, and I were mighty thankful, but Little Man only looked joylessly at his candy cane and stuck it into his shirt pocket.

'What's this?' asked Mr Tom Bee. 'What's this? Ain't ya gonna eat that candy cane, boy?'

Little Man shook his head.

'Well, why not? Mighty good!'

'Don't want they ole candy canes! They said I was dirty! I ain't dirty, Mr Tom Bee!'

Mr Tom Bee put his hands on his hips and laughed. 'Lord have mercy! Course ya ain't, boy! Don't you know them Wallace boys ain't got no more good sense'n a **wall-eyed** mule! Last thing in the world ya wantin' to be doin' is listenin' to anything they gotta say! They say somethin's red, ya best be figurin' it's green. They say somethin' dirty, ya gotta know it's clean! Shuckies, Little Man! You got more sense with them six years a your'n than them two boys ever gonna see. Don't ya never pay them no mind!'

Little Man thought on that, looked around at Stacey, who nodded his agreement with Mr Tom Bee, then took the candy cane from his pocket and gave it a **listless** lick.

Then Mr Tom Bee noticed Jeremy and snapped. 'You the kinda boy keep hold to yo' promises?'

Jeremy, who seemed taken aback by the question, nodded **mutely**.

At that, Mr Tom Bee pulled forth another candy cane and held it out to him. The boys and I waited, wondering if Jeremy would take it. Jeremy seemed to be wondering if he should. He hesitated, looked around as if fearful someone other than we would see,

---

wall-eyed: cross-eyed
listless: unenthusiastic
mutely: silently

and took it. He didn't actually say thank you to Mr Tom Bee, but then the nod he gave and his eyes did. I had a feeling Jeremy didn't see much penny candy either.

As Mr Tom Bee, the boys, and I started down the road, Jeremy called after us. 'Stacey! May – maybe one-a these here days, maybe I go fishin' with y'all . . .'

'Yeah . . .' Stacey replied. 'Yeah, one-a these days, maybe so . . .'

We headed on towards Aunt Callie's. Stacey sucked thoughtfully at his candy stick, then looked up at Mr Tom Bee. 'Mr Tom Bee, something I been thinkin' on.'

'What's that, boy?'

''Bout how come you to call Mr Wallace plain-out by his first name. I mean you don't call him mister or nothin'.' He paused. 'Don't know nobody else to do, nobody coloured I mean. Fact to business, don't know nobody coloured call a white man straight to his face by his first name.'

Mr Tom Bee laughed. 'He call me straight-out Tom 'thout no mister, don't he now?'

Stacey nodded. 'Yes, sir, that's a fact, but that's the way white folks do. Papa say white folks set an awful store 'bout names and such. He say they get awful **riled** 'bout them names too. Say they can do some terrible things when they get riled. Say anybody call a white man straight out by his name just lookin' for trouble.'

'Well, that's **sho** the truth all right,' agreed Mr Tom Bee. 'But shuckies! I ain't studyin' they foolish way-a things and I ain't gonna be callin' that John Wallace no mister neither! He done promised me long time ago

riled: angry
sho: certainly

I could call him straight out by his name long's I lived an' I aims to see he holds to his promises.' He paused, then added, 'Sides, we used t' be friends.'

'Friends?' said Stacey as if he didn't understand the word.

'That's right. Me and that John Wallace, we goes way back. Long ways back. Why, shuckies! I done saved that boy's life!'

We all looked up from our candy canes.

'That's right!' he said with an **emphatic** nod. 'Sho did! That John Wallace wasn't no more'n fifteen when I come along the road one day and found him sinkin' in swampland and pulled him out. Asked him what his name was. He said, call me John. So's that what I called him, jus' that. John. But that there was only the first time I done saved his life.

'No sooner'n I done him outa that swampland, I come t' find out he was burnin' up with fever, so's I doctored him. Ain't never laid eyes on the boy before, but I doctored him anyways. Doctored him till I got him well. Turned out the boy ain't had no family round here. Said he was coming up from down Biloxi way when he landed hisself in that swamp. Anyways, I let him stay on with me till he got hisself strong. Let him stay on long's he wanted and that was for quite some while, till the white folks round started meddlin' 'bout a white boy stayin' wit' me. I done took care-a John Wallace like a daddy woulda and long's he stayed with me, he minded what I said and was right respectful.'

Stacey shook his head as if finding that hard to believe.

---

emphatic: firm

Mr Tom Bee saw the disbelief and assured him it was so. 'That's right! Right respectful, and all that time, I been callin' him John. Jus' that. John. Well, come the day John Wallace tole me he was goin' up to Vicksburg to look for a job an' I said to him I figured next time I see him, I 'spected I'd most likely hafta be callin' him *Mister* John. And he told me things wasn't never gonna be that way. He says to me, I'm John t' you now, gonna always be John t' ya, cause you been like a daddy t' me an' I couldn't never 'spect my daddy to go callin' me mister. He done promised me that. Promised me he wasn't never gonna forget what I done for him. Said he was gonna always owe me. But then he come back down in here some years later to set up that store and things had done changed. He 'spected all the coloured folks to call him "Mister" John, and that there done included ole Tom Bee.'

'Owww,' I said, 'Mr John Wallace done broke his word!'

'He sho done that all right! Now I been thinkin' here lately maybe it's time I makes him keep his word. I figures I'm close 'nough to meetin' **my Maker**, it don't much matter he like it or not. I ain't studyin' that boy!'

I took a lick of candy. 'Well, Big Ma – she say you gonna get yourself in a whole lotta trouble, Mr Tom Bee. She say all them years on you done made you go foolish –'

'Cassie!' Stacey rebuked me with a hard look.

I gave him a look right back. 'Well, she did!' Not only had Big Ma said it, but plenty of other folks had too. They said Mr Tom Bee had just all of a sudden up and

---

my Maker: God

started calling Mr Wallace John. He had started after years of addressing John Wallace like the white folks expected him to do. Most folks figured the only reason for him to do a fool thing like that was because he had gone forgetful, but his advancing years were making him think it was a long time back when John Wallace was still a boy. I told it all. 'Said you just full of foolishness callin' that man by his name that way!'

Mr Tom Bee stopped right in the middle of the road, slapped his thighs, and let go a rip of a laugh. 'Well, ya know somethin', Cassie? Maybe yo' grandmama's right! Jus' maybe she sho is! Maybe I done gone foolish! Jus' maybe I has!'

He laughed so hard standing there, I thought he was going to cry. But then after a few moments he started walking again and the boys and I got right into step. Still chuckling, Mr Tom Bee said he couldn't rightly say he hadn't been called foolish before. In fact, he said, he'd been called foolish more times than he wanted to remember. Then he began to tell us about one of those times, and the boys and I listened eagerly. We loved to hear Mr Tom Bee tell his stories. With all his years, he had plenty of stories to tell too. He had seen the slavery days and he had seen the war that ended slavery. He had seen **Confederate** soldiers and he had seen **Yankee** soldiers. He had seen a lot of things over the years and he said he'd forgotten just about as much as he remembered. But as we walked the road listening

Confederate: soldiers of the southern states in the American Civil War (1861–5)
Yankee: soldiers of the northern states in the American Civil War (1861–5)

to him I for one was mighty glad he had remembered as much as he had.

We reached Aunt Callie's, gave her the head medicine and the fish, then headed back towards home. Mr Tom Bee was still with us. He lived over our way. To get home we had to pass the Wallace store again. When we reached the crossroads, Mr Tom Bee said, 'Y'all wait on up jus' another minute here. Done forgot my tobaccie.' A truck and a wagon were now in front of the store. Mr Tom Bee took note of them and stepped onto the porch.

Jeremy Simms was still sitting on the porch, but he didn't say anything to us this time. He nodded slightly, that was all. I noticed he wasn't sucking on his candy cane; I could see it sticking out of his pocket. He bit his lip and looked around uneasily. We didn't say anything to him either. We just stood there wanting to get on home. It was getting late.

Mr Tom Bee entered the store. 'Ey there, John!' he called. 'Give me some-a that chewin' tobaccie! Forgot to get it I was in before.'

The boys and I, standing by the gas pump, looked into the store. So did Jeremy. His father, Mr Charlie Simms, was in there now, sitting at the table by the stove along with his older teenage brothers, R.W. and Melvin. Dewberry and Thurston Wallace were there also and two white men we didn't know. They all turned their eyes on Mr Tom Bee. Dewberry and Thurston glanced at their father, and then Mr Charlie Simms spoke up. 'Old nigger,' he said, 'who you think you talkin' to?'

Mr Tom Bee wet his lips. 'Jus' . . . jus' come for my tobaccie.'

Mr John Wallace glanced at the men, then, his jaw hardening, set eyes on Mr Tom Bee. 'You bes' get on outa here, Tom.'

Mr Tom Bee looked around at the men. His back straightened with that old, sharp-edged stubbornness. 'Well, I sho do that, John,' he said, 'soon's I get me my tobaccie.'

Mr Simms jumped up from the table. 'John Wallace! You jus' gonna let this here old nigger talk t' ya this-a way? You gon' let him do that?'

Suddenly Stacey bounded up the steps to the store entrance. 'We – we waitin' on ya, Mr Tom Bee!' he cried shrilly. 'We waitin'! Come on, Mr Tom Bee! Come on!'

Mr Tom Bee looked over at him. He took a moment, then he nodded and I thought he was going to come on out. But instead he said, 'Be right wit' ya, boy . . . Soon's I get me my tobaccie.' Then he turned again and faced John Wallace. 'You – you gonna give me that tobaccie, John?'

Dewberry pulled from the counter. 'Daddy! You don't shut this old nigger up, I'm gonna do it for ya!'

Mr John Wallace turned a mean look on his son and the look was enough to silence him. Then he looked around the room at Mr Simms, at R.W. and Melvin, at Thurston, at the two other white men gathered there. The store and all around it was plunged into silence.

Mr Tom Bee glanced nervously at the men, but he didn't stop. He seemed bent on carrying this thing through. 'Well?' he asked of John Wallace. 'I'm gonna get me that tobaccie?'

Silently John Wallace reached back to a shelf and got the tobacco. He placed it on the counter.

Mr Simms exploded. 'What kind-a white man are ya, John Wallace, ya don't shut his black mouth? What kind-a white man?'

Mr Tom Bee looked at Mr Simms and the others, then went and picked up the tobacco. 'Thank ya, John,' he said. 'Jus' put it on my charges there, John. Jus' put it on my charges.' He glanced again at the men and started out. He got as far as the steps. The boys and I turned to go. Then we heard the click. The explosion of a shotgun followed and Mr Tom Bee tumbled down the steps, his right leg ripped open by the blast.

The boys and I stood stunned, just staring at Mr Tom Bee at first, not knowing what to do. Stacey started towards him, but Mr Tom Bee waved him back. 'Get 'way from me, boy! Get 'way! Stacey, get them younguns back, 'way from me!' Stacey looked into the store, at the shotgun, and herded us across the road.

The white men came out and sniggered. Mr John Wallace, carrying the shotgun, came out onto the porch too. He stood there, his face solemn, and said, 'You made me do that, Tom. I coulda killed ya, but I ain't wantin' to kill ya cause ya done saved my life an' I'm a Christian man so I ain't forgetting that. But this here disrespectin' me gotta stop and I means to stop it now. You gotta keep in mind you ain't nothin' but a nigger. You gonna learn to watch yo' mouth. You gonna learn to address me proper. You hear me, Tom?'

Mr Tom Bee sat in silence staring at the bloody leg.

'Tom, ya hear me?'

Now, slowly, Mr Tom Bee raised his head and looked up at John Wallace. 'Oh, yeah, I hears ya all right. I hears ya. But let me tell you somethin', John. Ya was

John t'me when I saved your sorry life and you give me your word you was always gonna be John t' me long as I lived. So's ya might's well go 'head and kill me cause that's what ya gon' be, John. Ya hear me, John? Till the Judgement Day. Till the earth opens itself up and the fires-a hell come takes yo' ungrateful soul! Ya hear me, John? Ya hear me? *John! John! John!* Till the Judgement Day! *John!*'

With that he raised himself to one elbow and began to drag himself down the road. The boys and I, candy canes in hand, stood motionless. We watched Mr John Wallace to see if he would raise the shotgun again. Jeremy, the candy cane in his pocket, watched too. We all waited for the second click of the shotgun. But only the cries of Mr Tom Bee as he inched his way along the road ripped the silence. '*John! John! John!*' he cried over and over again. 'Ya hear me, John? Till the Judgement Day! John! *John! JOHN!*'

There was no other sound.

The Mirror
Eiko Kadono

Eiko Kadono was born in Tokyo, Japan, in 1935. She has written many tales for young people and has won several awards for her writing. In this thought-provoking short story, she explores some of the issues surrounding appearance and reality.

Although a mirror reflects outward appearances, in this story, Eiko Kadono reminds us that there is often a lot more to people than meets the eye . . .

As you read, *think about the two characters of the girl Ariko. Are they really separate people or are they different sides of the same person? How far do you change your behaviour depending on your mood or the people you are with?*

'Mum! Have you see my new hat?' I called loudly, rushing downstairs.

'You were trying it on in front of the mirror last night, weren't you, Ariko?'

I looked into the next room on the way down, but my hat wasn't there. Where could it be? If I didn't hurry, I'd miss the bus. I had to be there, waiting, when Hiroshi arrived.

On the way home from school the other day, Hiroshi and Isamu were walking in front of me. I quietly moved closer to them and I could hear Hiroshi talking.

'On Sunday, I'm going to the video games shop in Machida. Why don't you come along, Isamu? Second-hand games are really cheap there, you know. Come on, keep me company for a change,' he insisted.

'No, I don't think I can,' Isamu said, looking unhappy.

'How come?'

'No money.' Isamu grimaced to cover his embarrassment, and started to run off. 'Maybe some other time. See you later!' He waved and disappeared round the corner.

Hiroshi snorted in disappointment and broke into a trot.

Watching him go, I made up my mind that I would go to the video games shop in Machida. I knew where that shop was. I'd go and wait in front of it and, when Hiroshi arrived, I'd act surprised and pretend it was a coincidence. My heart began to pound at the thought.

Hiroshi was the tallest boy in our class. He was quite handsome and had long eyelashes, like the heroes in the comic books we were always reading. The girls never took their eyes off him, especially Keiko and Yasuko. Whenever they could find the time, they seemed to be gossiping about him.

Of course I was no exception. I too was drawn to Hiroshi. I decided I wouldn't tell anyone I was planning to go to Machida. Little by little I'd make friends with Hiroshi and then secretly, unknown to everybody, I'd have him all for myself. Then, when the secret got out, wouldn't everyone be surprised! I could almost hear them whispering about it now. I was nearly dancing on air at the very thought of their reaction.

On Sunday, I thought, I'll wear my dress with the red polka dots and the white hat Mum bought me. I'll blow-dry my hair to make it silky and bouncy, the way I like it best.

So last night I'd done a little rehearsal, putting on the hat and turning this way and that. Mum had a knowing smile on her face when she said to Dad, 'I'm glad I bought that hallway mirror, now that we have a stylish girl in the house. After all, she's already twelve.'

'I suppose so,' Dad said with a frown, 'but I get a scare when I open the front door late at night and come face to face with myself.'

'The truth about Dad,' I said **melodramatically**, 'is in the mirror! Maybe what surprises you is the reflection of what you really are. There must be something suspicious about you,' I teased him. 'Suppose what surprises you is the mirror showing what you really are? . . . No, I'm only joking! Just joking,' I protested as Dad glared at me.

But I couldn't help feeling I was right.

Mum's eyes twinkled as she said **chidingly**, 'Goodness, Ariko, you shouldn't talk like that to your father.' She turned to Dad. 'Dear, I'm sure you'll get used to the mirror after a while.'

'Well, Dad,' I said, 'if you don't like being welcomed home by the spooky mirror, come home earlier – while Mum and I are still awake.' And I went back to admiring myself. Yes, I thought, preening myself, I do look pretty cute.

That was only last night, and now the hat was nowhere to be seen. Could I have left it on top of the chest of drawers in my room? I started to run back upstairs to check again, but something stopped me. It was me,

---

melodramatically: in an exaggerated way
chidingly: scolding

reflected in the mirror, but grinning, with a **snide** sort of smile. That's strange, I thought, and then I caught my breath. The me in the mirror was holding the hat.

'Oh, there it is!' I exclaimed and, without thinking, I stretched out my hand. Suddenly my hand was grasped and tugged so that my whole body was pulled forward into a spin and then thrown out somewhere.

'Mum, I found my hat, so I'm going.'

It was the girl with the hat who spoke, and she was moving towards the front door.

'Wait, wait!' I called out, my arms flailing desperately.

Looking back, the girl smiled wryly and said, 'Sorry about that,' and then she ran out of the door.

That was *my* face, no mistake. But . . . why? I'm *here*.

My mum's cheerful farewell echoed down the hallway. 'See you later! Take care now.'

I didn't understand what was happening. But then I thought, I have to go after that girl and stop her.

I got up, but immediately I ran full force into some obstacle. I moved forward again, and again I hit something. I couldn't get through. Yet the hallway and the rest of the house were right there in front of me. I could see the back of the sofa where we sat to watch television and, past that, the front door. To one side was the kitchen, where Mum was washing the dishes.

'Mum! Mother!' I screamed, beating at the barrier wildly with my fists. But she didn't even turn around. I tried again, throwing my whole weight into the effort. But I bounced back and crumpled into a heap. Gasping, I huddled there for some time.

---

snide: sly

Mum turned around, wiping her hands on her apron, and came up to the mirror. She brought her face close to the glass.

'Mum, it's me! Here!'

Again I pounded at the mirror. But Mum obviously couldn't see or hear me. She looked at herself, smoothing an eyebrow with her forefingers and pursing her lips as if putting on lipstick.

Then suddenly I realised where I was. I was inside the mirror! I must have been pulled in when my arm was tugged, a little while before. But whoever had heard of a person being inside a mirror? If I really was inside the mirror, the girl with the hat must have pulled me in. Yet that girl's face was unmistakably my own. If that was me, why was I here? And who was that girl?

Mum went upstairs, humming, and soon she came back down, dressed to go out. I could hear the front door open and the key turn in the lock outside. Through a slit in the curtains, I caught a glimpse of her, walking towards the main street. It was Sunday. Dad should be home, I thought. No, now I remembered: he had gone out early in the morning to play golf.

I began to think that if I'd got into the mirror, there must be a way out. I began to fumble at the invisible wall in front of me, but I suddenly realised in horror that I could not see my own hands. I raised both arms and stared hard, but I couldn't see them. Alarmed, I looked down at my feet. They were invisible. My heart began to pound and the blood drained from my head.

'No! Oh, it can't be true! Help me!' I began to scream hysterically, groping frantically to touch different parts of my body. I could feel them there, my arms, my chest

– I just couldn't see them. All I could see was an inky blackness.

I looked behind me. It was black there, too: total darkness. I couldn't even see my shadow. I was completely alone and scared. Was I going crazy? On the other side, the room outside the mirror was bright, but not a ray of light from that side shone into my side of the mirror.

Finally I heard the noise of the key turning in the lock and the front door being flung open.

'How come it's so hot in here? I can't stand it!'

The girl lunged through the door and dropped the hat on a chair, grabbing the air-conditioner's remote-control. She stood in front of the cool air that was streaming forth, raising and flapping her skirt to let in the breeze. She didn't seem to care that her pants were showing. She got herself a drink of water from the kitchen and came over to the mirror, sticking her chin out at me meanly.

'Well, aren't you looking the frightened one!' she exclaimed.

'What? You can see me!' I said.

'That's right. Once I'm on this side, you can see me – yourself – but if I don't come up close, you can't see the real you. It's all up to me whether you see yourself or not!'

I tried holding up my hand again. Now I could see my palm shining whitely in the darkness. I quickly checked again. Now I could see my feet and knees and stomach. With a rush of relief I felt for my arms.

'If you want to be able to see yourself, you have to treat me better, you know. Hey! Listen, there's something

I want to tell you. I did go to Machida and met Hiroshi instead of you. Everything went just fine. Don't worry about a thing.' She spoke with sneaky tone in her voice.

'I don't care about that. Just get me out of here!' I shouted, thrashing about.

'No, don't go getting yourself all worked up!' she said, her mouth forming a crooked grin. 'I'm going to hang around out here for a while. I'm going to change your whole life. I'll make your sweetie-pie life even more sweetie-pie . . .'

'I don't need your help! Just what is going on, anyway? What are you trying to do? Come on, explain. Why am I here, anyway?'

'I grabbed your hand on purpose.' She giggled meanly, showing her open palm and slowly waving it. 'You're so dimwitted, you obviously didn't realise it, but every time you looked in the mirror you totally ignored me. You only saw what you wanted to see, posing like a "good girl!" all the time, even though in fact you're really shamelessly self-centred. People may pat you on the back and praise you, but it makes *me* sick. I was horrified every time I saw you acting like that. I made up my mind to give you a hard time when I got the chance.'

'That's no concern of mine. It doesn't make sense! Now, get me out of here straight away!'

'One of these days . . . maybe, some time,' she said haughtily. 'When I think it's time, I'll let you out. So you'd better just wait quietly until then. What're the tears for? Well, that's a new one – when did I ever see you crying before? Do you think you can scare me by crying, young lady? Whether you get out or not is up to *me*. All I have to do is take hold of your hand.'

'OK, then, quick! Come on, please!' I didn't want to admit that I was at her mercy, but I stretched out my right hand.

'I'd never take your hand now, silly, I just got here! I finally broke loose of you! So I'm not about to give you my hand any time soon.' She hid her hands behind her, then she took first one and then two steps away from the mirror, smiling all the time.

Mum came through the front door. 'Oh, Ariko, you're back already. That was a quick trip. Wasn't it hot out there today?' Taking a deep breath, Mum put a large shopping bag on the sofa. 'Did you have fun in Machida?'

'Nothing special,' the girl replied in a sullen voice.

'Did you buy anything?'

'Nothing in particular.'

'That doesn't tell me much. You did have a good time, I hope. Who did you go with?'

The girl didn't answer.

'Ariko. I asked you a question . . .'

'What does it matter who I went with? It has nothing to do with you, Mum. Why do you ask so many questions?' The girl made no attempt to hide her snort of contempt.

Mum's hand stopped on the way to the refrigerator door. She turned in amazement to stare at her.

'Ariko, dear, what happened to you?'

'I said, "Nothing in particular." It was fun enough.' The girl threw me a look and then, to change the subject, poked her hand into Mum's shopping bag.

'What did you buy . . . wow! You bought me that blouse, didn't you?'

I could hear her ripping the paper bag open and pulling out a light-blue blouse, she pranced towards the mirror, posing with it in front of her.

'What do you think? Isn't it nice?' she said to me in a low voice as she modelled the blouse.

It was a beautiful colour. Mum must have bought the blouse because she knew I had wanted something in that colour for a long time.

'Show me,' I said, putting my hands out in front of me.

'Here.' She started to hold up the blouse close to the mirror, but then in a flurry she snatched it back. 'Oh! Oh, no you don't! That was close!' She quickly drew back, and turned away in the other direction.

'So, do you like it?' Mum asked.

'Mum, you know I don't like this colour. It's like any old blouse. Go back and change it for something more flashy.' Her tone was petulant, totally different from a moment ago when she had stood, showing off her prize, in front of me.

'What, you don't like it?' Mum was taken by surprise.

'I'm so bored with this colour. Everything's this blue. I'm not a kid any more, you know.' Throwing the blouse at Mum, she stumped noisily up the stairs. Shocked and speechless, Mum didn't move for a moment.

'Goodness, what's happened to her?' she said softly, gazing after her. Once, talking on the phone to a friend, Mum had said, 'Ariko's never been a problem. Well, she's caught a cold now and then, maybe, but we always get along. My husband teases us for being like twins.' Now, that confidence was gone. She looked bewildered at the sudden change in her daughter.

Mum started to make coffee. I wondered what I had done to deserve such a cruel turn of events. Tears welled up in my eyes. I hadn't felt hungry since morning and I didn't have to go to the bathroom, but for some reason my tears kept flowing.

Enveloped in darkness, I huddled there like a baby, clasping my knees, and sobbed.

'You should just give up.'

The sudden sound of a voice speaking in the darkness was eerie. At once distant and very close, it sounded like a boy's voice.

'Who are you?' Startled, I straightened and looked around. Again I asked, this time with more urgency in my voice, 'Who is it? Answer me!'

'My name is Kazuo.'

'Where . . . where are you?'

'Right here, beside you.'

'Where? I can't see a thing.'

'No, I'm invisible.'

'But you can see me, right?'

'No.'

'Oh, no! Until just a minute ago, I could . . .' My voice trailed off as I saw that my body had disappeared again.

'You can see yourself only when she stands in front of the mirror. When we enter here, we have no form,' the boy's voice explained.

'What do you mean, "when we enter here"?' I was trembling from head to foot. 'You mean you, too, were pulled into the mirror?'

'Yes. Yes, but it was a long time ago.'

'What do you mean, "a long time"?'

'It'll be about twenty-five years now.'

'What! Did you say twenty-five years? Oh, no!' I let out a scream.

'Wow! You've still got feelings.' Kazuo was chuckling. He sounded a little less eerie than before. The voice now was that of an ordinary boy, but it had no expression, like someone reading tonelessly from a book.

'In my case, it was a test paper. I'd got a really bad report, and just as I was about to tear it up so my mother wouldn't find it, the me in the mirror grabbed it. When I lunged after it, he pulled me in.'

'He looked just like you?'

'Yeah, exactly. Except he was a really good kid.'

'So you've been in here ever since? No, that just can't be! You must be making this up.'

'I wish it weren't true . . . But unfortunately, I am still here. He was very careful. Saying all the while that he'd let me out eventually, he never held his hand out even once. Then, six years later, he was run over by a train and killed. I've remained the same age ever since – I don't age, no matter how much time passes. Probably I can't even die. And there is no chance I'll ever be able to cross back to the other side. Pretty depressing story, huh?'

'But there was your mother. Didn't she help you?'

'Hardly,' he snickered. 'She had my other side right there with her. And besides, he was suddenly such a smart, good boy. He didn't talk back or misbehave. Day in, day out, Mother looked so happy. She was overjoyed with her son. So when he died, you should have seen how she grieved. My father had died, and I don't remember him at all. Around three years after that, my mother remarried – a guy from the place where she worked. And she moved out, leaving this old mirror behind.'

'Just a minute!' I was beside myself, trying to think what that meant. 'You mean you've been in here ever since?'

'I can't even see my mother.'

I turned back towards the house in which I had been moving about freely until this very morning. The rays of the evening sun were shining through the clouded glass in the front hallway. Mum was at the kitchen sink, starting to make dinner. I could hear the sound of water running and Mum humming as she worked.

'Mum! Mum!' My tears gushed out.

'You're lucky you can still cry,' Kazuo said. 'After a while it gets hard to talk, and you forget words.'

'Oh, no! Not me!' I said desperately. 'I'm getting out of here. No matter what it takes.'

'Well, you'll have to beg that girl for it,' Kazuo said.

Mopping up my tears with my skirt, I raised my head. There were a lot of things I wanted to ask this boy, Kazuo.

'So you must have come into my house with this mirror.'

'That's right. But I've been all over the place. After a while, the person who bought my house sold the mirror to an antiques dealer. From there it was bought first by a boutique and later by an actress, then by some kind of scholar. And then by the antiques shop where your mother bought it. I moved every time a house was redecorated or rebuilt.'

'And are you the only one left inside like this?'

'Actually, there was someone else. A girl. The daughter of the scholar. By the way, how old are you?'

'Twelve.'

'That's what I thought. You know, it's really strange. That girl was twelve, too. And I was twelve.'

'And what happened to that girl?'

'Strange things started to happen, and then . . .'

'Like what?'

'The girl out there started acting oddly. She stopped talking to the others in the family – or to anybody. She stopped going to school. She'd just sit in front of the mirror and daydream, but carefully, keeping her hands well away. And then, at night, she'd look in the mirror, put on lipstick, and then get up and go out somewhere. Her mother and father would forbid her, but she'd go anyway, and she **raised a ruckus** if they tried to stop her . . . Come to think of it, I just realised while I was telling you all this – the ones on the other side of the mirror all go crazy in some way or other. In my case, he got run over by a train, the scholar's daughter went mad – and that girl who took your place is pretty weird, too.'

'But yours was a good boy, wasn't he? Did you say he was really smart?'

'Yes, he looked just like me but, unlike me, he was really clever, and he was nice to my Mum and everything. But then one day, when he saw the train coming, he jumped off the platform and started walking towards the train, all very calm and smiling. That's not normal, you know. So everyone said it was suicide. Maybe there was something, something that went haywire inside that kid. That's the only explanation I can think of. And that girl, you know, she was really a sweet-looking, good kid, and then she

---

raised a ruckus: created a scene

suddenly started acting crazy like that. She threw a marble clock at her father and hurt him.'

'You're kidding!' I remembered the cold, **non-committal** answers the girl had made to my mother's questions earlier, the way she seemed to have a chip on her shoulder. Then suddenly I felt a cold shiver run down my spine. 'So what happened to that girl? Where is she?'

'Her parents decided they'd better put her in a different school. Eventually it was decided that they would move to her mother's home in the country, and they disposed of all their household furniture. On the day they handed the mirror over to the antiques dealer, the girl out there turned her back without so much as a look in our direction, and left. The girl on this side cried and screamed with all her might, but there was nothing she could do. And so we were handed over to the antiques shop.'

'And then what happened? She's obviously not here any more.'

'Well, for about ten days she went on crying. But gradually she calmed down and then finally, murmuring, "I'm going, I have to see if there's anything out there," she disappeared. I tried to stop her, but . . . I wondered why she went. At least here we can see the goings-on in the world outside. She might even see her **counterpart**, or her family, again one day. My me isn't around any more, but I believe something might happen that could free me from the mirror. Help can only come from that bright world, so I'm waiting for my

---

non-commital: neutral
counterpart: other half

chance. After all, I really belong to the world out there.'
He paused and then went on. 'If you sit very still in this
darkness, you begin to think you can hear something.
When the house is quiet, try listening. From somewhere
deep, deep down, it sounds as if many people are
calling out to each other. The sound is very faint,
though. I think that girl was drawn away by that sound,
and I sometimes think I'll just give up and walk away
from here – I've even taken a step or two into the
darkness. But you have to be really brave, you know –
it's pitch black! It's so scary – and you might melt into
nothingness in the dark. I just can't do it.'

'No! No! No!' I began to cry again, blubbering out
loud. 'I'm only twelve! I want to move around out there
in the bright light!'

'I envy you, still being able to cry.'

'What, you can't cry?'

'You can cry because there are still people you love
out there, people you can see and hear. When you
don't have anyone . . . You know, I'm really glad you
came; I feel some warmth coming back into my body.'

I could hear the sound of long suppressed tears and
a faint sniffling. By now Kazuo's voice was almost back
to normal.

'Hey! Hey, you-who-is-me.' The voice was coming from
somewhere above, and I looked up.

'You're looking pretty pale and **wan**. All tired out, eh?
Well, let me tell you, you've got a long wait ahead of
you, so get a grip on yourself.' She shook her head and
with a proud gesture ran her fingers through her hair.

wan: worn-out

I was totally exhausted. Three days had passed. Now and then that girl would come up to the mirror, just like before, and tease and mock me. Each time I strained every nerve as I watched for the chance to grab her hand, but the effort left me weary.

'You know, today Hiroshi is coming here,' she announced.

'Where?' I doubted my ears.

'Here, to the house. I invited him to tea,' she said coyly. 'See how clever I am. I used my head, I can tell you. The difference between you and me, you know, is here and here.' She pointed first to her heart and then to her head.

'If Keiko or Yasuko knew, wouldn't they be surprised! And to think, they have a crush on him!' she snickered.

The doorbell rang.

The girl ran over and opened the door. Hiroshi came in through the door. I could see his face over her shoulder. Tight-lipped and with eyes glaring, he looked extremely tense.

'Oh, come on in,' the girl said.

'I haven't come just for fun,' Hiroshi said. 'I came to set things straight.'

'Set what straight?'

'That I'm not going to spend any more time with you.'

'Well, that's pretty final.'

'I almost decided not to come, but I think you ought to know how I feel about this.'

'What are you talking about?'

'I did no such thing as try to steal something at the games shop. You said if I didn't come over here, you'd spread the story around school that I have been shoplifting. But I didn't do it!'

'Ha! You're lying. Don't you remember we agreed to do it together?' Her body swayed slightly.

Hiroshi's eyes flashed. 'When did we ever agree to do anything? I never thought you were such a troublemaker, Ariko.' His voice rose to a shout. 'How can you do such a thing?'

The girl's voice rose to match his. 'You can shout all you like, but I know you're really a coward.'

'Ariko! What's going on?' Mum's voice called from upstairs.

'Nothing, Mum.' The harsh siren suddenly turned into the sweet daughter. 'Hiroshi's come over to visit.'

'I'm leaving.' Hiroshi turned away.

'OK, you can go home. But I'll see you tomorrow at school, and you'd better be prepared.'

'For what?' He turned back towards her, glaring.

'What on earth is the matter?' Mum was coming down the stairs. 'Quarrelling? My goodness, you're not little kids any more.'

Trembling with anger, Hiroshi appealed to my mother. 'Mrs Mori, Ariko's gone too far. I won't let her get away with it. Listen to what she did. The other day I went to the video games shop in Machida, and as I passed the cash register an alarm went off. Somehow, a game I hadn't paid for had got into my bag, and the shopkeeper accused me of shoplifting. But I tell you, Mrs Mori, I didn't do it. I don't do things like that! Then I saw Ariko on the other side of the shop. Since I knew Ariko from school and I thought she was nice, I hoped she'd help me get out of this mess. But do you know what she did? She said, "I'm sorry. We agreed to do it together. I took one too," and she pulled a game out of her pocket. And then she started weeping and saying,

"Hiroshi kept saying, 'Let's do it, let's do it,' until I . . ." But listen, Mrs Mori, I absolutely did not do it. How can she do such a thing to me!'

'Hiroshi, how can you lie like that?' the girl shouted. 'You were the one who said, "Let's do it together – I always do it, so it'll be OK." How can you put all the blame on me like that? You're the one who's the coward!'

'What in heaven's name . . .' Mum looked stunned, as if her face had frozen. In the mirror, too, I was so surprised I thought I'd stopped breathing. To say that Horishi had shoplifted! Never. I knew he'd never do such a thing.

Hiroshi continued, 'I've been to that shop many times and the shopkeepers knew me, so they went easy on us. The manager said, "I suppose you two just couldn't resist. We'll let you off this time, but next time we'll call the police." And after really bawling us out, they let us go.

'But then today at school, Ariko told me she was going to tell everybody. I told her that, if she did that, I'd tell them about her too. But then she said, "Oh! I didn't do anything! What, are you going to lie again?" She's crazy. I won't believe a word she says. And then she says if I don't want the story to get out I have to tell everybody that I'm in love with her and am going to visit her at home. Over my dead body – I'll never say anything like that! The whole thing is crazy!'

'Ariko. Is all this true?' Mum's voice was trembling.

'Do you think I'd do anything like that, Mum? Hiroshi's just lying,' the girl said, trying to look innocent.

'I am not lying,' Hiroshi declared firmly.

'OK, OK. So why don't you go on home? So, I won't

tell on you. I won't say you were a thief. OK?' She made it sound as if she was doing him a favour.

'I didn't do it!' he shouted again, **incensed**.

Mum's voice was trembling. 'Hiroshi, Ariko's not been herself lately. She's suddenly become very angry all the time, and I've been rather worried about her myself.'

'There's nothing wrong with me,' the girl snapped.

'I'll talk things over carefully with Ariko later, Hiroshi, so could you forget about this for today? Ariko, tell him you're sorry.'

'No!'

'Ariko!' Mum's voice rose in warning.

'OK, I guess there's no end to this. I'm going home.' He sounded a little calmer as he ran out.

On the verge of tears, Mum turned to the girl. 'Ariko, what is the meaning of all this? I can't believe you would do such a thing. Even if somebody encouraged you to do it, I could never believe that you would shoplift.'

'So you believe Hiroshi instead of me, Mum? So that's how it is, is it? I think I have a headache. I'm going to bed.' And the girl set off up the stairs.

'Wait! Just wait a minute, Ariko!'

Mum stared into the girl's face. With a penetrating look, she said, 'Are you really Ariko? You're acting like someone completely different . . .'

'I'm your daughter, all right? If you hate me so much, slap me, or you can even kill me. It happens all the time.' She spat this out and then ran up the stairs. I could hear the sound of my bedroom door slamming. Mum sank down, exhausted, where she was and gazed upwards as if to hold back the tears that brimmed in her eyes.

---

incensed: furiously angry

I felt as if my heart would break. Just who could that girl be? That girl who looked exactly like me – she had called me 'You-who-is-me' . . . What could she have meant?

Then Dad came home. Coming home from work he was almost always too late to join us for dinner, and it was unusual for all three members of our family to eat together. Both Mum and the girl were silent.

Dad was in a good mood. 'Wow! Beef stew! Mum's stew is the best. This makes me want some wine. Would you bring us a bottle, dear?'

Gazing nervously at the girl, Mum slowly replied, 'That's a good idea. Ariko, you're closest could you bring over the wine?'

'Bring it yourself,' she snapped with disdain.

Darting a startled look at Mum, Dad turned to the girl. 'What's the matter with you? Here we are, about to enjoy a meal together for a change, and you act like this. Come on, let's try to enjoy ourselves, OK?'

'You say "for a change". Don't you think it's asking too much for you to leave us alone all the time and then come back and be treated nicely? Yes, it's been a long time since we ate together, so don't you think you should be a little more humble?' She rolled her eyes spitefully.

Dad's face flushed and his hands began to tremble. 'How dare you talk to me like that!'

'All right. I'll shut up. I'll do anything you say. I'm just here to follow your orders. Isn't that right? It's a real nightmare, eating with this kind of family!' Slamming her chopsticks down on the table, she stood up and made for the stairs.

Dad stood up to go after her, but then he stopped, his eyes following her. He didn't really believe what he had just witnessed.

Mum tried to **intercede**. 'Now, dear, let's keep calm. Why don't you sit down? She's at a difficult age, you know. And you're not completely free of blame yourself.'

'What? How am I to blame?'

'Well, don't you always tell us you have to "work, work, work"? You never take time to be with Ariko these days. When was the last time you talked to her at all?' Mum's voice gradually grew more accusing.

'That's nonsense! It's my job – to support the two of you!' Now Dad was getting angry.

'You always say it's for our sakes, but how do you know that's what we want most of all? I can't think of anything that takes us more for granted. If being out every night of the week and spending your weekends with your company friends is for our sakes, you don't have to do it any more for us. It's no wonder Ariko's started misbehaving. Today at school she threatened a friend in the most unthinkable way. It's terrible!'

'So you've both decided it's all my fault. I left everything in the household up to you, believing that you were capable of handling it. Have I ever complained about the way you ran things? Haven't I left you to do exactly what you wanted, free to use the money I earned in the way you saw fit? Did you ever consult me before you bought something? Take that gloomy old mirror. I don't care whether it's an antique or whatever you make it out to be, but I don't like it.'

---

intercede: make peace

'Well, excuse me, but it was you, by the way, who said it would be nice to have a mirror in the hallway. I just acted on your suggestion. Oh, never mind, I'll phone the shop tomorrow and have them take it back.'

'You do whatever you want.' Dad got up noisily, shuffled into his shoes, and left the house.

How could things have reached such a pass? Ever since that girl had pulled me into the mirror, something seemed to be wrong with both my mother and father. Now it looked as if the whole household was going haywire. Suddenly I felt myself going very cold all over. Mum's words came back to me: tomorrow she would call and have the mirror taken away. This mirror!

'Kazuo! Kazuo!' I called out in a panic, searching around me in the darkness.

'I'm right here,' the voice said, very near me.

'Mum says she's going to return the mirror to the shop.'

'Yes, I heard.'

'Where will I be taken? If I'm separated from that girl, I'll never get out of here.'

'Yes, that's true.'

'Isn't there something I can do? Come on, tell me!'

'If I knew, I wouldn't be here . . .'

'But he died. There's no one to pull you back anyway.'

'I wish you'd have a little more respect for my feelings.' Kazuo sounded hurt. 'Now listen, no matter how much you scream and carry on, what can't be done can't be done. People go their separate ways, or die, eventually. You're old enough to know that.'

'Oh, no!' I collapsed, crying.

Then I heard Mum talking on the phone. 'I'm sorry to cause you so much trouble, but you know the mirror I bought the other day? I wonder if you'd be willing to take it back? My husband says it's too big, you see. At half the price? That would be fine. Tomorrow? I'll be at home in the morning. Fine. I'll be waiting.'

After putting down the receiver, Mum turned around and looked long and hard at the mirror. Her face was **haggard**, with circles round her eyes and sunken cheeks. In the space of only one day, her face had undergone unbelievable changes.

Suddenly the girl was standing in front of me. 'Did you know? They're going to return this mirror to the shop?'

I nodded silently.

'I'd like to do you the favour of changing places, but *I* don't want to go back in there either.' She threw out her arms and shrugged. 'That's the way it is. Put up with it, OK?'

Her attitude made me mad. I felt as if my blood would boil, but I tried to keep my feelings in check. I said calmly, 'Which one of us will have to put up with it, I wonder. The family is a mess anyway. It's going to break apart. Mum and Dad aren't getting along. And then there's you, with your heart as black as the devil. You're going to go on living like that, with everyone in the family on a different wavelength, sniping at each other all the time. Good luck!'

'Black as the devil, you say? Hah! I won't be a kid for ever, you know. I'll manage all right.'

'That's impossible! Because you took over everything!'

---

haggard: hollow, strained

The girl turned away sullenly. 'Don't act so superior.' She tried to laugh at me, but her face suddenly betrayed fear and it lost its look of spitefulness. 'I didn't want to take over. I just wanted to get away from you for a change – to find out what it would be like without you,' she murmured as if talking to herself.

Morning came. I crouched down and put my face on my knees, gazing intently at the house, visible before me. I could hear the sound of the newspaper man's bicycle. The sun began to shine through the kitchen window and gradually spread through the rooms.

Mum came down the stairs and started to make breakfast. She was making coffee. She was frying eggs. I realised that these ordinary things, that had been such a routine part of my day, no longer would be.

Mum made her own breakfast only and began to eat. Dad came down, ready to go to work. He left without saying a word to her.

Then the girl came down the stairs. 'I'm not going to school today,' she said.

'Please yourself,' Mum said sharply.

'Hello!' a man called, peering in at the door. 'I've come to take the mirror.'

'There it is, if you wouldn't mind taking it down,' Mum said.

'I'm sorry if you didn't like it, ma'am. It's very old but a first-class mirror, the kind of thing you don't find much any more.'

'Yes, but my husband said he didn't like it, and when he says something like that, there's no changing his mind.' She didn't smile.

The man stared for a moment in amazement, but then he got hold of himself. He slipped off his shoes to enter the house and crossed the hallway to unfasten the mirror.

I braced myself and then called out, 'Kazuo!'

There was no answer, only the huge shadow of the man blocking my view of the house. He raised his arm and began to unscrew the mirror from the wall. I could hear the sound of the screws turning.

Then I saw the girl watching. From a distance, but watching, her eyes flicking this way again and again, she was looking but pretending not to.

Gathering all my strength, I screamed, 'Do you really want it to end like this?' But she turned away quickly and hid behind the wall. The mirror shifted and was taken off the wall and set on the floor.

'Kazuo! I'm . . . I'm leaving, I'm going,' I shouted.

This time he answered. 'Don't go! You mustn't go! If you go, you could miss your chance. That other girl never did come back. It's better to stay here. And you never know who else might come in. It might get to be quite lively in here. Please stay!'

'No! I can't stand it. Even if I stay, what good is it? Did you see her, she just abandoned me, as if it meant nothing to her at all! I give up on her. It doesn't matter what, I have to get out of here.'

I closed my eyes, took a deep breath, and plunged into the darkness.

'Don't leave me all alone again!' Kazuo's voice trailed after me.

For a moment I thought my body had melted into the darkness. It was deep, seemingly liquid. Nothing moved. But from far, far away, I thought I could hear something: voices mingling, whispering, murmuring, seemed to call to me. I felt as if I had melted and was flowing towards those faint sounds. So it is all over, I thought, I am going to be blotted out.

Then, little by little, I felt something stirring near me. It was like a breeze, a faint current of air, and then, far, far ahead, a tiny point of light appeared. Hastily, as if gathering up lost parts of myself, I tried to find my body. I could feel myself. I even felt a little strength. Relying on the warmth of that strength, I struggled to wade through the darkness towards that point of light. I was determined to reach it.

The ray of light gradually broadened and then grew stronger, lighting up my surroundings slightly. There – I could see the gate of our house. The front door, the door was open. The man in overalls carrying the mirror out of the door. I started running.

'Wait! Could you just wait a minute, mister!' The girl's cry from inside the house was close to a scream, and then she flew out of the door. I ran, holding my right hand out in front of me. She came running, her hand held out. Our hands touched and gripped. We came back together again.

The antiques shop dealer said, 'Oh! Miss. What is it? Did you forget something?'

'Oh! Oh, no, nothing. Thank you,' I answered. She answered.

That night, my father came home early. He opened the wine himself and poured some for Mum too.

Oh, it's delicious!' Mum took one sip and let her breath out. 'I guess you're right. It's better not to have a mirror there in the hall. It was kind of **oppressive**, as if one was always being watched.'

'See, that's what I meant. But never mind. I'll buy you a better one, one of these days,' Dad said, as if nothing had happened.

But I said, 'I don't need a big mirror there. The one in the bathroom is enough for me.'

I checked my mum's face and then my father's. Nothing seemed to have changed. But I had seen the other side of my mother and father. I knew that I would go on living with this mother, this father, and that girl who was the other side of myself.

About a month later, I happened to pass by the antiques shop. When I peered into the shop, the shopkeeper saw me.

'Have you sold that mirror already?' I asked, my heart fluttering a bit.

'Yes. It was a good mirror. I put on a new frame and sold it very quickly. Would you have liked it, young lady?'

'No, no. I was just curious.' I backed out politely and walked away quickly.

So, now where had Kazuo gone? Had he ever gone into the darkness? Wherever he was, I couldn't help feeling he was right here, quite close to me. Kazuo would be watching over me from now on. I would always think that, even though I couldn't see him.

Now, whenever I see a mirror, I just put my hands behind my back. I never want to be pulled in there again. But then, I'll never be twelve again either.

---

oppressive: threatening

Once Upon a Time

Nadine Gordimer

This is a disturbing and grim story inspired by Nadine Gordimer's experience of apartheid in South Africa where people were separated according to the colour of their skin. The story addresses the instability, suspicion and violence that result from this kind of system. It reads like a fairytale, but there is nothing happy and carefree about what happens in this house . . .

As you read, *think about the writer's claim that this is a children's story. Does this seem like a children's story to you? Are there issues in this that you think children should know about?*

Someone has written to ask me to contribute to an anthology of stories for children. I reply that I don't write children's stories; and he writes back that at a recent congress/book fair/**seminar** a certain novelist said every writer ought to write at least one story for children. I think of sending a postcard saying I don't accept that I 'ought' to write anything.

And then last night I woke up – or rather was wakened without knowing what had roused me.

A voice in the echo-chamber of the subconscious?

A sound.

A creaking of the kind made by the weight carried by one foot after another along a wooden floor. I listened.

---

seminar: class

I felt the **apertures** of my ears **distend** with concentration. Again: the creaking. I was waiting for it; waiting to hear if it indicated that feet were moving from room to room, coming up the passage – to my door. I have no burglar bars, no gun under the pillow, but I have the same fears as people who do take precautions, and my windowpanes are thin as **rime**, could shatter like a wineglass. A woman was murdered (how do they put it) in broad daylight in a house two blocks away, last year, and the fierce dogs who guarded an old widower and his collection of antique clocks were strangled before he was knifed by a casual labourer he had dismissed without pay.

I was staring at the door, making it out in my mind rather than seeing it, in the dark. I lay quite still – a victim already – the **arrhythmia** of my heart was fleeing, knocking this way and that against its body-cage. How finely tuned the senses are, just out of rest, sleep! I could never listen intently as that in the distractions of the day; I was reading every faintest sound, identifying and classifying its possible threat.

But I learned that I was to be neither threatened nor spared. There was no human weight pressing on the boards, the creaking was a buckling, an **epicentre** of stress. I was in it. The house that surrounds me while I sleep is built on undermined ground; far beneath my bed, the floor, the house's foundations, the **stopes** and

---

apertures: openings
distend: get wider
rime: coating of ice
arrhythmia: unsteady beat
epicentre: central point of an earthquake
stope: mine dug in steps

passages of gold mines have hollowed the rock, and when some face trembles, detaches and falls, three thousand feet below, the whole house shifts slightly, bringing uneasy strain to the balance and counterbalance of brick, cement, wood and glass that hold it as a structure around me. The misbeats of my heart tailed off like the last muffled flourishes on one of the wooden xylophones made by the Chopi and Tsonga migrant miners who might have been down there, under me in the earth at that moment. The stope where the fall was could have been disused, dripping water from its ruptured veins; or men might now be **interred** there in the most **profound** of tombs.

I couldn't find a position in which my mind would let go of my body – release me to sleep again. So I began to tell myself a story; a bedtime story.

In a house, in a suburb, in a city, there were a man and his wife who loved each other very much and were living happily ever after. They had a little boy, and they loved him very much. They had a cat and a dog that the little boy loved very much. They had a car and a caravan trailer for holidays, and a swimming pool which was fenced so that the little boy and his playmates would not fall in and drown. They had a housemaid who was absolutely trustworthy and an **itinerant** gardener who was highly recommended by the neighbours. For when they began to live happily ever after they were warned, by that wise old witch, the

---

interred: buried
profound: deep
itinerant: travelling

husband's mother, not to take on anyone off the street. They were inscribed in a medical benefit society, their pet dog was licensed, they were insured against fire, flood damage and theft, and subscribed to the local Neighbourhood Watch, which supplied them with a plaque for their gates lettered YOU HAVE BEEN WARNED over the silhouette of a would-be intruder. He was masked; it could not be said if he was black or white, and therefore proved the property owner was no racist.

It was not possible to insure the house, the swimming pool or the car against riot damage. There were riots, but these were outside the city, where people of another colour were quartered. These people were not allowed into the suburb except as reliable housemaids

and gardeners, so there was nothing to fear, the husband told the wife. Yet she was afraid that some day such people might come up the street and tear off the plaque YOU HAVE BEEN WARNED and open the gates and stream in . . . Nonsense, my dear, said the husband, there are police and soldiers and tear-gas and guns to keep them away. But to please her – for he loved her very much and buses were being burned, cars stoned, and schoolchildren shot by the police in those quarters out of sight and hearing of the suburb – he had electronically-controlled gates fitted. Anyone who pulled off the sign YOU HAVE BEEN WARNED and tried to open the gates would have to announce his intentions by pressing a button and speaking into a receiver relayed to the house. The little boy was fascinated by the device and used it as a walkie-talkie in cops and robbers play with his small friends.

The riots were suppressed, but there were many burglaries in the suburb and somebody's trusted housemaid was tied up and shut in a cupboard by thieves while she was in charge of her employers' house. The trusted housemaid of the man and wife and little boy was so upset by this misfortune befalling a friend left, as she herself often was, with responsibility for the possessions of the man and his wife and the little boy, that she implored her employers to have burglar bars attached to the doors and windows of the house, and an alarm system installed. The wife said, She is right, let us take heed of her advice. So from every window and door in the house where they were living happily ever after they now saw the trees and sky through bars, and when the little boy's pet cat tried to climb in by the fanlight to keep him company in his little bed at night, as it customarily had done, it set off the alarm **keening** through the house.

The alarm was often answered – it seemed – by other burglar alarms, in other houses, that had been triggered by pet cats or nibbling mice. The alarms called to one another across the gardens in shrills and bleats and wails that everyone soon became accustomed to, so that the din roused the inhabitants of the suburb no more than the croak of frogs and musical grating of **cicadas'** legs. Under cover of the electronic **harpies'** discourse intruders sawed the iron bars and broke into homes, taking away hi-fi equipment, television sets, cassette players, cameras and radios, jewellery and clothing, and sometimes were hungry enough to devour everything in the refrigerator or paused **audaciously** to drink the whisky in the cabinets or patio bars. Insurance companies paid no compensation for single malt, a loss made keener by the property owner's knowledge that the thieves wouldn't even have been able to appreciate what it was they were drinking.

Then the time came when many of the people who were not trusted housemaids and gardeners hung about the suburb because they were unemployed. Some **importuned** for a job: weeding or painting a roof; anything, ***baas***, madam. But the man and his wife

---

keening: wailing
cicada: grasshopper-like insect
harpies: winged monsters in Greek mythology
audaciously: boldly
importuned: pleaded
baas: master

remembered the warning about taking on anyone off the street. Some drank liquor and fouled the street with discarded bottles. Some begged, waiting for the man or his wife to drive the car out of the electronically-operated gates. They sat about with their feet in the gutters, under the **jacaranda** trees that made a green tunnel of the street – for it was a beautiful suburb, spoilt only by their presence – and sometimes they fell asleep lying right before the gates in the midday sun. The wife could never see anyone go hungry. She sent the trusted housemaid out with bread and tea, but the trusted housemaid said these were loafers and ***tsotsis***, who would come and tie her up and shut her in a cupboard. The husband said, She's right. Take heed of her advice. You only encourage them with your bread and tea. They are looking for their chance . . . And he brought the little boy's tricycle from the garden into the house every night, because if the house was surely secure, once locked and with the alarm set, someone might still be able to climb over the wall or the electronically-closed gates into the garden.

You are right, said the wife, then the wall should be higher. And the wise old witch, the husband's mother, paid for the extra bricks as her Christmas present to her son and his wife – the little boy got a Space Man outfit and a book of fairy tales.

But every week there were more reports of **intrusion**: in broad daylight and the dead of night, in the early hours

---

jacaranda: tropical flowering tree
tsotsi: no-good person
intrusion: forced entry

of the morning, and even in the lovely summer twilight –
a certain family was at dinner while the bedrooms were
being **ransacked** upstairs. The man and his wife, talking
of the latest armed robbery in the suburb, were
distracted by the sight of the little boy's pet cat
effortlessly arriving over the seven-foot wall, descending
first with a rapid bracing of extended forepaws down on
the sheer vertical surface, and then a graceful launch,
landing with swishing tail within the property. The
whitewashed wall was marked with the cat's comings and
goings; and on the street side of the wall there were
larger red-earth smudges that could have been made by
the kind of broken running shoes, seen on the feet of
unemployed loiterers, that had no innocent destination.

When the man and wife and little boy took the pet
dog for its walk round the neighbourhood streets they
no longer paused to admire this show of roses or that
perfect lawn; these were hidden behind an array of
different varieties of security fences, walls and devices.
The man, wife, little boy and dog passed a remarkable
choice: there was the low-cost option of pieces of
broken glass embedded in cement along the top
of walls, there were iron grilles ending in lance-points,
there were attempts at reconciling the **aesthetics** of
prison architecture with the Spanish Villa style (spikes
painted pink) and with the plaster urns of **neo-classical
façades** (twelve-inch pikes finned like zigzags of

---

ransacked: turned upside-down
aesthetics: visually attractive qualities
neo-classical: like the architecture of Ancient Greece and
Rome
façades: fronts

lightning and painted pure white). Some walls had a small board affixed, giving the name and telephone number of the firm responsible for the installation of the devices. While the little boy and the pet dog raced ahead, the husband and wife found themselves comparing the possible effectiveness of each style against its appearance; and after several weeks when they paused before this barricade or that without needing to speak, both came out with the conclusion that only one was worth considering. It was the ugliest but the most honest in its suggestion of the pure concentration-camp style, no frills, all evident **efficacy**. Placed the length of walls, it consisted of a continuous coil of stiff and shining metal **serrated** into jagged blades, so that there would be no way of climbing over it and no way through its tunnel without getting entangled in its fangs. There would be no way out, only a struggle getting bloodier and bloodier, a deeper and sharper hooking and tearing of flesh. The wife shuddered to look at it. You're right, said the husband, anyone would think twice . . . And they took heed of the advice on a small board fixed to the wall: Consult DRAGON'S TEETH The People For Total Security.

Next day a gang of workmen came and stretched the razor-bladed coils all round the walls of the house where the husband and wife and little boy and pet dog and cat were living happily ever after. The sunlight flashed and slashed, off the **serrations**, the **cornice** of

---

efficacy: usefulness
serrated: cut like a saw-blade
serrations: tooth shapes
cornice: top layer of a wall

razor thorns encircled the home, shining. The husband said, Never mind. It will weather. The wife said, You're wrong. They guarantee it's rust-proof. And she waited until the little boy had run off to play before she said, I hope the cat will take heed . . . The husband said, Don't worry, my dear, cats always look before they leap. And it was true that from that day on the cat slept in the little boy's bed and kept to the garden, never risking a try at **breaching** security.

One evening, the mother read the little boy to sleep with a fairy story from the book the wise old witch had given him at Christmas. Next day he pretended to be the Prince who braves the terrible thicket of thorns to enter the palace and kiss the Sleeping Beauty back to life: he dragged a ladder to the wall, the shining coiled tunnel was just wide enough for his little body to creep in, and with the first fixing of its razor-teeth in his knees and hands and head he screamed and struggled deeper into its tangle. The trusted housemaid and the itinerant gardener, whose 'day' it was, came running, the first to see and to scream with him, and the itinerant gardener tore his hands trying to get at the little boy. Then the man and his wife burst wildly into the garden and for some reason (the cat, probably) the alarm set up wailing against the screams while the bleeding mass of the little boy was hacked out of the security coil with saws, wire-cutters, choppers, and they carried it – the man, the wife, the hysterical trusted housemaid and the weeping gardener – into the house.

---

breaching: breaking through

The First of my Sins
Brian Friel

This interesting and humorous story by the Irish writer Brian Friel looks at the way adult behaviour can sometimes seem very puzzling and unfair to children. It describes a boy's worries as he approaches his first confession, as part of the Catholic ceremony of confirmation.

As you read, *notice how realistically the writer creates the character of David. Despite all his 'sins', what makes him come across as an innocent child?*

I can recall the precise moment in my childhood when I had the first **intimation** of the real meaning of sin. It occurred on a Friday evening in the June of my eighth year, the day before I made my first confession. Mother and I had had a row – it ended with mother shouting. 'You are nothing but an animal – a dirty, little animal!' and slapping my face – and I had run, bawling, out of the house and down to the bank of the stream that flowed past the foot of our garden. I remembered I was wearing my new shoes to break them in for the next day, and in my blind rush through the garden I had stepped into a cake of cow-dung. That finished me altogether. A slap on the face merely pricks one's pride but cow-dung on new shoes shatters one's dignity. I flung myself on the ground and was screaming my head off when I felt a hand on my shoulder and heard

---

intimation: warning

Uncle George's voice behind my neck. I was aware that he was trying to console me in his awkward way but I kept up my screaming for a time to **establish** my wretchedness. He got down on his knees beside me and asked what had happened. I told him. He raised me into a sitting position on the bank – I was then at the sniffling stage – and pulled handfuls of grass, and began wiping the manure off my new shoes, and all the time he talked and talked, no doubt to distract me, about the great city of London where he lived and about the Royal Majestic Hotel where he worked. I did not understand half of what he was saying, but his voice was soft and comforting, and I was content just to listen. And it was then, when he was telling me about his job as night porter, that I had the sudden, **momentary intuition** of what sin really is. I will not pretend that I knew fully – for that matter, I am still far from certain – but there, on the bank of that yellow stream listening to Uncle George rambling on as if he were talking to himself, I got a flicker of real understanding, and that lightning **intelligence** was so different to what I had been taught by Sister Benignus, my teacher, or by Father Clancy, who examined our **catechism** lessons, or by mother, who had me gurgling prayers before I could walk, so different but so illuminating, that I felt suddenly very wise and very crafty and very old.

---

establish: make clear
momentary intuition: brief sense
intelligence: knowledge
catechism: question-and-answer text on the Roman Catholic religion

Uncle George had appeared out of the blue a fortnight before, and as soon as I saw him I was disappointed. I imagine he was about fifty then, tall and loose and ungainly, and when he walked his shoulders and arms worked **in unison** with his feet so that, with every step he took, one side of his body swivelled forward. His face was pale and disturbed every so often by a muscular twitch in his right cheek which drew his features into a quick, unhappy smile. His eyes were shy and constantly on the move in case, if they rested for any length on one place, they might see anything. I knew from mother, his sister, that he had run away to sea as a boy and that he had travelled the world, and night after night I had dreamed of him and his great **exploits**. And I might have forgiven him his appearance if he had told me tales of high adventure and mutiny and pirates. But this great **loping** giant, who arrived unannounced one morning and who spent his days tramping around the Tyrone countryside, seldom spoke, and I never saw him except at meal times when he ate **voraciously** and smiled his bleak involuntary smile at father's persistent **banter**. I told any of my friends who asked me about our visitor that he was suffering from shell-shock.

Everybody assured me that my first confession would be the happiest day of my life, a day I would always remember; and as that Saturday drew near life certainly became more and more blissful. Father

---

in unison: in time with, on the same side as
exploits: deeds
loping: with a long stride
voraciously: greedily
banter: light-hearted conversation

bought me a new bicycle. Mother got me a new suit and new shoes. Auntie Mary sent me £1 and Auntie Kathleen 30/- (it was her privilege, as my godmother, to outdo Auntie Mary). Sister Benignus gave me a pair of **rosary beads** and Father Clancy presented me with a white prayer book, inscribed 'To a great little man' (I considered the description accurate and could not understand why it brought tears to mother's eyes). Indeed I was beginning to wonder what further ecstasy confession itself would bring when on the eve of the big event mother and I had the row and I was plunged into despair – and dung.

We had got the half-day off school that Friday afternoon, and when I went home I found mother ironing my new suit to smooth out the shop creases. I jumped up on a stool on the other side of the ironing board and watched. The next day was suddenly very close to us.

'You go to church at ten?' mother said.

I nodded my head.

'Will Sister Benignus be there?'

I said she would.

'I suppose you know what you're going to tell the priest, David?'

'Of course!' I said.

'Of course,' she said.

'Bless-me-Father-for-I-have-sinned. Please-Father-this-is-my-first-confession. Please-Father-I . . .'

'No, no no, David. Don't tell me. That is something for the priest alone. I don't want to hear your sins.'

30/-: £1.50 in pre-decimal money
rosary beads: strung beads used to keep count of prayers

'I don't care,' I said **indifferently**. 'I told Sister Benignus.'

'Did you?'

'We all did. You know – a sort of practice.'

'Yes?'

'She just laughed at me.'

'Laugh? Why did she laugh?'

'How would I know?' I said.

She hung the jacket on a coat hanger and spread the trousers on the board. 'You must have said something that made her laugh.'

'I told her what I'm going to tell the priest: Please-Father-this-is-my-first-confession. Please-Father-I-killed-a-cat-once. That-is-all-Father.'

Mother smiled across at me. I thought for a second she was going to kiss me. But she went on ironing. 'Yes, that was a naughty thing to do, killing that cat. And you're sorry, aren't you?'

'In a way. But it ate Roger.' Roger had been my pet rabbit.

'Still, you're sorry you killed it?'

'I suppose so,' I said. I put my cheek on the warm surface of the ironing board and remembered Roger.

'David, don't you think you should mention to the priest what happened last Tuesday week?'

'Mm?'

'I can't talk to you lying down like that. Sit up.'

I sat up.

'I said should you not tell the priest what happened last Tuesday week?'

'When was that?'

---

indifferently: without concern

'The day we went to see Auntie Mary.'

'Did I do something wrong?'

'Don't you remember?' she said. 'She and I were having a cup of coffee and you crawled under the table. Remember?' She was using the tone of voice she used when we had visitors.

'What did I do?' I was genuinely interested.

'Well,' she said, 'you crawled under the table – she and I were sitting, chatting – and you crawled under the table – and – and – and you pulled up her skirt.'

'Oh, that!' I said, disappointed.

'You did, you know, David.'

'I only wanted to see the colour of her knickers. I told you that.'

'I know. I know. But still . . .' Her face was flushed with the heat of the iron. 'And I merely mention it now, David, in case you think you might like to tell the priest about it. It was – it was a naughty thing to do.'

'That was no sin!'

'It was naughty.'

'Sister Benignus told me it was no sin. So there!'

Mother looked quickly at me. 'Told you? Did you ask her?'

'Course I did. Because I knew I was right and you were wrong.'

'What did you say to her?'

'I told her,' I said patiently, 'that I pulled up Auntie Mary's skirt to see what colour her knickers were, and that she squealed, and that you wouldn't speak to me all the way home in the bus. And I asked her was it a sin.'

'And what did she say?'

'She said, "Run away and have a bit of sense. She's easy made squeal." That's what she said. So there!'

'No need to make a face at me, David,' mother said. 'I'm only trying to help you.'

But I knew she was annoyed with me. Her mouth had gone tight. 'And there's another thing,' she said.

'Another what?'

'That fight you had with Tony Brennan last Monday. Don't you think you should tell that to the priest tomorrow?'

'Tell what?'

'That you hit Tony with your fist.'

'That was no sin!'

'Did I say it was, David?'

'You said I should tell the priest. Why should I tell him if it wasn't a sin?'

'I'm merely suggesting things you might have overlooked, things I myself might consider telling if I were you.'

'It was his fault. He hit me first.'

'Two wrongs don't make a right. And, anyhow, you must have made him angry.'

'He wouldn't kiss me,' I explained. She thought I said 'kick'.

'And why should he kick you, for heaven's sake?'

'I didn't say kick – I said kiss! We were all kissing each other. Billy Kerrigan and Eamonn Shine and Paul Shiels and Sean O'Donnell, and Tony wouldn't join in. And when I tried to make him he hit me and I hit him back.' I knew by her face that she did not understand.

'I told you before!' I said. 'You must have forgotten!'

'No,' she said softly. 'You never told me why he hit you in the first place.'

'Anyhow, we're pals now again,' I said.

'When – when did this happen, David?' she asked, smoothing very slowly.

'What?'

'This – this kissing.'

'In the toilets. At lunchtime.'

'Yes?'

'Well, that's all. It was just a game. And Tony got angry.'

'A kissing game?'

'Not the way you kiss,' I said, because I could see that she still did not understand. 'This was fun kissing – you know? – just touching tongues. And when I went to Tony with my tongue out he wouldn't put out his tongue because he said my tongue was dirty. And then he hit me because I was going to make him kiss me.' She did not speak. 'So I hit him back,' I concluded.

'I think you should mention that to the priest, David.'

'What?'

'What you have just told me, the whole thing exactly as you have told me.'

'That was no sin!'

'David, it is the priest's job to advise you on what is right and what is wrong. He might think that this – this game is not a nice game for young boys.'

'The kissing game?'

'Whatever you call it,' she said.

'I'm not going to tell him about the games we play!' I said stoutly.

'I think you should, David. He will be able to tell you if it is wrong.' She paused. 'Yes. Tell him exactly as you told me and then ask his advice. Father, you'll say, is this – this game we play sinful or not.' She began working briskly again. 'Now, we have a real confession to make, haven't we? First, we killed the cat. Second, we looked up Auntie Mary's skirt. And third, we played this – this kissing game – with other boys. Don't you agree? Are you listening to me, David? I said don't you agree?'

I should have said yes just to satisfy her and then gone ahead with the confession I had rehearsed. But some stubbornness, some vague sense of independence, took possession of me.

'No,' I said sullenly.

'No – what?'

'The cat is the only thing I'm going to tell.'

'David – '

'I told you why I pulled up her skirt: I just wanted to see the colour of her knickers!' I was shouting in self defence. 'And the kissing game was only a game, and I hit Tony because he hit me! That was no sin either! And I'm not going to tell things like that to the priest!'

'David, if your mother tells you to –'

'Father Clancy said it in school. The priest wants to hear nothing but your sins, he said; he doesn't want to hear what you had for your breakfast or how far you can spit. That's what he said.'

'I'm telling you, David, that there are certain things –'

'I don't care what you say. I know! Father Clancy told us!'

'How dare you speak to me like that!'

Now the two of us were shouting. 'I'll tell about the cat but I'll tell nothing else! I won't! I won't!'

'David!'

'I won't! I won't! I won't.'

We both got the smell of burning at the same time.

'Oh, God!' said mother, snatching up the iron. But the damage was done. A brown triangle, the shape of the iron, was imprinted on the seat of my new trousers.

'Oh, God!' mother groaned. 'Your suit's ruined! Ruined!' Suddenly her anger overflowed. 'And it's all your fault, you little brat, you!' It was then she slapped my face with her open hand. 'D'you know what you are?' she shouted. 'You're nothing but an animal – a dirty little animal!'

And that was why I had run, bawling, out of the house and down to the bank of the stream where Uncle George found me, and wiped the manure off my feet, and comforted me with his soft voice, and distracted me with his rambling conversation.

There are times when I imagine I remember every detail of that scattered **soliloquy**, when I think I can recall everything that Uncle George said to me. But I know I cannot. What I do remember, vividly, is the drowsy heat of the evening sun, and the noise of the stream, and the smell of grass and dung, and the bleak flitting smile on his face, and his glancing looks at mine. And I remember, too, parts of what he said.

He had held dozens of jobs, he told me, all over the world – docker, insurance man, sailor, mechanic, prospector, labourer, soldier; and always he had left them because – and I have no doubt about the expression he used – 'because people were always bribing you, smiling and bribing you at the same time.' I asked him about his job as night porter in the Royal Majestic Hotel and he told me that he had left it, too, because people kept slipping him money and winking at him and squeezing his elbow. 'Do you see?' he kept saying. 'Do you see? Do you see? Do you see?'

---

soliloquy: talking to oneself

repeating the **staccato** words again and again so that I tried, tried desperately, to understand him. I cannot have understood. But, young as I was, I got an inkling of what he was trying to tell me: that evil abounded, all over the world; and that evil-doers were people who smiled, and somehow, with their smiles and their sly intimacy, involved others in their **corruption**; and that one had to keep going from place to place and from job to job to avoid being corrupted by them.

'There,' he said, jumping to his feet. 'Those shoes are cleaner now, aren't they?'

I looked at them. 'Mother wanted me to stay off the grass,' I said. I was on the verge of tears again.

'Tell you what,' he said. 'Go back to the house; and go up to my room, and in the case under the bed you'll find a pair of brushes and a tin of polish. Give the shoes a good rub and they'll look as good as new.'

'You come with me,' I said.

The muscle twitched and the eyes slid all over the place. 'I think I'll go for a walk,' he said. 'You go ahead. Under the bed. In the case. Okay?' And off he strode as if he were being followed.

Because I was nervous of meeting mother I slipped in the back door and went cautiously up to Uncle George's room. I found the cardboard case and the brushes in it and cleaned my shoes. They looked as good as new. Then, when I was putting the brushes back, I noticed a small bundle, covered with newspaper, in the corner of the case. I felt it. It was hard. I tore a corner off the paper and stuck a finger

---

staccato: jerky
corruption: dishonesty

into the hole. The finger found a smooth, cold surface. My curiosity was too strong: I opened the parcel. It contained six knives and six forks and six spoons, each with the letters RMH on the handle. My Uncle George had stolen them! My Uncle George was a thief!

Mother ignored me when I went down to the kitchen. She moved from the cooker to the table and back to the cooker, and brushed past me as if I were not there.

I asked when tea would be ready.

'You owe me an apology, David,' she answered.

'Sorry,' I said dutifully.

'I hope you are,' she said. 'Any boy about to make his first confession and shouting at his mother like that! Shame on you!' Usually when we had a row, she kissed me when we made it up. But that day she told me to stop hanging around and make myself useful.

I did all the little jobs that always merited a hug: I set the table for her; I carried in the extra chair from the sitting-room; I brought in coal for the night. But still she froze me. I could endure it no longer. I had to have her affection.

'Do you want to hear a secret?'

'If you wish to tell me,' she said.

'It's a big secret,' I said temptingly.

She did not speak.

'It's the biggest secret I ever had,' I said.

'If you're going to tell me, then tell me. If you're not, run upstairs and leave out fresh underclothes. You're having a bath after tea.'

I **sidled** over to the cooker and stood beside her. 'I'll tell you,' I said.

---

sidled: edged

'What is it? What is it?' She did not even look at me.

I hesitated for a moment, long enough to weigh the **revelation** I was about to make against her warm love which I hoped to win in exchange. I made the choice.

'Whisper,' I said. She stooped down to me.

'Uncle George is a thief,' I said into her ear. 'His case is full of knives and forks and spoons that belong to the London hotel!'

Through the wall that separated my bedroom from the living-room I heard the row that night. Father spoke occasionally, **placatingly**, and Uncle George did not speak at all; it was mother who made all the noise. She shouted and sobbed and moaned, and the words 'disgrace' and 'thief' pierced into me again and again. It kept on for a long time and then there was silence. But still I did not sleep. Then I heard Uncle George moving about in his room upstairs and then the front door was opened and shut and then there was no more sound.

Mother woke me with a kiss and said gently, 'David, darling, do you know what day this is?' It was a glorious June morning. I had a special breakfast in the dining-room (I usually ate at the kitchen table) and mother attended to me as if she were a waitress.

Then we walked hand-in-hand to the church and on the way we met Billy Kerrigan and his mother, and Paul Shiels and his mother, and Sean O'Donnell and his mother, each couple hand-in-hand just like mother and myself. All the mothers chatted away and we smirked at one another in embarrassment.

---

revelation: announcement
placatingly: trying to make peace

We stopped at the door of the church. Mother fixed my hair and pulled down my jacket so that the burn on the trousers was concealed. 'Ready?' she said.

'Is Uncle George gone away?' I asked.

'He is,' she said. 'Let's not talk about him.' She adjusted my collar. 'Remember our little chat yesterday?'

'Yes.'

'And the three things to tell the priest.'

'Yes.'

'And you're sorry for them?'

'Yes.'

'Good,' she said. 'Good boy. Now, in you go. I'll be waiting for you when you're finished.'

I took my place in the queue. When my turn came I went into the little box. I told the priest what I had done to Uncle George; and when he said, 'Is that all, son?' I told him again because he obviously did not understand the **enormity** of my sin. But he nodded his head and said, 'I know. I know. Is there nothing else?'

'No, Father,' I said. He gave me **absolution** and asked me to pray for him.

I came out into the golden church and walked towards the row of eager, smiling mothers kneeling at the back.

---

enormity: seriousness
absolution: forgiveness

The Guest

Leena Dhingra

Leena Dhingra was born in India, but has lived in many countries including France, England, India and Belgium. The teenager who describes the action in this story lives in both the English culture of her school friends and the Indian culture of her home. When Divya's Indian grandmother comes to England, she is far too friendly with strangers and Divya feels she must change her ways.

As you read, *think about how Divya sees the two cultures she lives in. Do you think she sees one as better than the other, or does she enjoy the advantage of having two different backgrounds?*

Ekadashi is the eleventh phase of the moon and a day on which many people observe a fast. My grandmother, whose name, Chand, means moon, has always fasted on that day. She started fasting when she was twenty to **commemorate** an event that changed her life. She told me about it all that summer. That summer when Mrs Collins came to stay.

It was the year of my lower sixth. My parents were to be away in New York for five months and had arranged for my grandmother from India to come and stay with me. I'd tried arguing that I could easily manage on my own, that I was seventeen after all and that people of my age left home, held jobs, lived independently and

---

commemorate: remember formally

even got married and produced families. Ravi, my elder brother, offered to come up from university every weekend. They just laughed us off, pronounced a little speech that, as a student, my responsibility was to study and theirs was to make sure I had the support to concentrate on my work! I let the matter slide. I knew from experience that what I called a discussion they would call an argument or rudeness. Like the time Mum let me go to assertiveness-training classes with Annie, and then said I was being rude whenever I tried to put into practice what I had learned. I complained to my friends Cheryl and Annie about the overprotectiveness of Indian parents and the injustice of it all.

Of course, deep down, I knew that they were right and I was really quite pleased that Chand-Nani, my grandmother, was coming. I just wasn't very good at listening to deep down in those days.

So Nani came with all her usual **paraphernalia**: her special milk pan, her herbal concoctions, her incense, her **murthis**, her **Gita**, her pictures, her prayer cushion, oil lamp, **Ganga water** and all the fragrant eccentricities that reminded me of India.

The first two weeks went off fine and we settled into our routines. We shared the cooking and other chores. She went for walks, visits, said her prayers and, as usual, went regularly to the Saturday jumble sales from where she **gleaned** nearly new clothes to take back to

---

paraphernalia: personal belongings
murthis: holy statues
Gita: Hindu god
Ganga water: holy water from the River Ganges
gleaned: picked up

India for 'the refugees'. This was a bit of a standing joke in the family. Nani herself had been a refugee and had lost everything in **the partition**. But even though that was years ago, she still collected clothes to distribute and would seek out the needy.

One weekend Ravi came up and, on the Sunday, Nani went to leave him at Victoria station. It was the day of her fast, when she had only one small meal of fruit in the evening. I was on my way to Annie's to revise when I realised that Nani had forgotten her keys. Obviously I couldn't go and was discussing notes on the phone when the doorbell rang. I opened it and

the partition: separation of India and Pakistan in 1947

there stood Nani with an odd-looking stranger – all mousy browns: grey-brown hair, brown felt hat, brown coat with threadbare patches, brown shoes with grey dust, and carrying a small brown case and a brown paper carrier bag. Standing next to my grandmother in her **ochre** silk sari and maroon woven shawl, she could not have presented a stronger contrast.

'So sorry, darling, I forgot my key. This is Mrs Collie, we met at Victoria station and I've invited her to come and stay with us for a while. Will you put the kettle on, sweetheart, and make us all a cup of tea? I'll just light my **jauth** and join you in the kitchen.' With this, Nani breezed past me, slipped out of her shoes and disappeared down the hall leaving us staring at each other.

'The name is Collins, Mrs Collins,' said the stranger stepping forward and **articulating** every syllable as though I didn't understand English.

I didn't realise my mouth was wide open until I had to close it to reply.

'I'm sorry. My grandmother does mispronounce . . .'

Mrs Collins darted a quick and critical glance over the hall, taking in the shoe rack, the coats, the pictures, the smudges around the door handles. In the kitchen, she pushed her bag and case under a chair, barricading them in with her legs and giving me a hostile look as she sat down. I put the kettle on and dashed off to find Nani in her room, sitting there all serene, folded palms, staring into the flame of an oil

---

ochre: yellowish-brown
jauth: oil lamp
articulating: pronouncing

lamp and counting her never-ending beads. She did this every morning and evening. I sighed loudly. When she had finished, she looked at me and just smiled through my indignant questioning.

'What's so strange? I told you. We met at Victoria station. She needed help – a place to stay – and so I invited her here.' Nani smiled, so **disarmingly**. Such a beautiful smile. 'It's just for two or three days, until she can find the friends she came to stay with.'

'But, Nani . . . one doesn't . . . we don't . . . we don't know her!'

'Do we really know anybody? Do we know ourselves? Think about it.' She looked at me strangely as though across a great distance. 'For the present,' she said mysteriously, 'Mrs Collie is our guest!'

Honestly! This is ridiculous I thought, but all I managed to say was: 'Her name isn't Collie. It's Collins. Collies are dogs like Lassie.'

Suddenly my grandmother whizzed out of the room apologising down the hall. When I reached the kitchen she and Mrs Collins were having a little **tête-à-tête**, as the kettle steamed away around them. It was really all too absurd.

I drifted back to my books and saw the telephone was still off the hook. Annie! What was I going to tell my friends?

By dinner, Mrs Collins was looking decidedly more at ease: her bags were now in a corner of the kitchen, she'd removed her hat, coat and shoes, was wearing Nani's slippers and inspecting the spices.

---

disarmingly: innocently
tête-à-tête: private conversation

'I was already **in service** by the time I was your age – seventeen, isn't it, dearie? Started at the bottom and worked my way to the top. I always had my standards, see. I'll give this kitchen a good scrub up after dinner.'

'Why? Is it so filthy?' I said, sitting down. Nobody seemed to notice.

'This is just a simple meal, Mrs Collins, and not too spicy.' Nani put the dishes on the table.

'Oh, don't worry about me. I can eat all sorts. Worked in the house of a man who'd been out in India. They had a native cook. They'd brought him back from India they had. He cooked all sorts – native food, English food. I ate everything. Never been fussy, I haven't.'

Suddenly, she leaped out of her chair, rummaged through her carrier and triumphantly pulled out a greasy brown paper bag. 'I nearly forgot. I've a pork pie here we can all share.'

'A pork pie!' I burst into a fit of nervous giggles, **anticipating** the consternation of my vegetarian grandmother – and on the day of her fast too. But Nani just took out the pie, put it on a plate, and even cut it with her own hands as though it was the most natural thing to do.

That evening when Nani requested me to be more polite, I challenged her. 'What politeness do you want? English politeness or Indian politeness?' I said. 'Do you want me to say please, thank you and sorry properly, or do you want me to **curb** my independent opinions?'

'What about just showing respect to another.'

---

in service: working as a domestic servant
anticipating: expecting
curb: control

'But she's . . .'

'She's our guest. And a guest is a god.'

'It's utterly unbelievable. I mean, you just wouldn't believe it,' I complained to my friends Annie and Cheryl. 'I explained to her that she could be from anywhere, that they were closing the asylums these days and that all sorts of people were wandering around in the streets. But she took no notice, just smiled.' Annie and Cheryl listened greedily. 'I mean, last night,' I continued, 'I got out of bed in the middle of the night because I could hear her creaking and shuffling around.'

'Where was she sleeping?'

'Well, Nani offered her the couch in the living-room, she looked around the room and then said, "No, it wouldn't be proper." So we put her on a camp bed in the hall. In any case, when I got there she was out of the bed and had crept into the living-room, and guess what she was doing?'

'What?'

'Well, she was going round to all the pictures, all the statues – you know, the dancing **Shiva**, the **Durga**, the **Krishna**, and all – and making the sign of the cross over them!'

'How odd!' exclaimed Annie.

'She probably thinks it's all the Devil's business. I've met people like that,' **intervened** Cheryl. 'You know, the commandments and all. **Graven** images. Some people take that all quite literally!'

Shiva, Durga, Krishna: Hindu gods
intervened: interrupted
Graven: carved

Before I could have my next burst of righteous indignation, Cheryl said, 'I think it's really kind of your Nan to help a stranger. Don't you agree, Annie?'

'Well, I suppose it is, if you look at it that way. But Dee is right. She could be from anywhere.'

That evening, when I came home, a makeshift clothes line had been erected by the kitchen window on which Mrs Collins's clothes were drying, the kitchen itself had been rearranged so as to provide a little cosy corner in the sun in which Mrs Collins was comfortably sitting in one of Nani's 'refugee' dressing-gowns, darning her stockings. As I slipped out of my shoes in the hall, I noticed that the kitchen floor looked as though it had been polished.

'There's fresh tea in the pot, dearie,' she called out. 'Your gran's out and said you're to study till she returns.'

I frowned, dropped my bags and came in to pour my tea. The floor had definitely been polished.

'And when you've finished you will dry the cup and put it away and not just leave it dripping on the draining board,' she said through her teeth as she tried to break the thread with them.

In my irritation I spilt some tea on the floor.

'Wipe it with the floor cloth, will you, dearie? It's over the bucket under the sink.' She said this without looking up, **pre-empting** my reaching for the dishcloth. I did as I was told.

'It's good to have standards,' she announced in a firm lilt as I left the kitchen, fuming with irritation.

When Nani came in, Mrs Collins melted all over her. 'Good evening, madam, let me take those bags, madam, and madam, do sit down, madam, and tea?'

---

pre-empting: preventing

Nani was all smiles, and her new, strange, distant look appeared to have acquired a kind of radiance.

That night again, the floorboards creaked as Mrs Collins crept around the house when she thought we were all asleep. She inspected the paintings, the statues, the books. She opened the drawers and cupboards. I warned Nani that when Mrs Collins left on Thursday one of us should be there when she packed. Nani just nodded but did not seem unduly concerned. So I felt that it was my duty to keep an eye on things and every night I crept around after her to try and see what she was up to. Once, I had to hide in the hall cupboard and wait until she was in her bed snoring before I could get out and climb back into mine. I went to sleep during French in school and was given a detention.

When I came back from school, Nani announced that Mrs Collins would be staying on because her friends hadn't yet returned. She was out collecting some of her things from some left-luggage place. Just like that!

I wrote to Ravi and told him he must come at once as there was an emergency.

That night, Mrs Collins got up as usual, and I crept after her. The living-room door was ajar and in the mirror above the fireplace I was greeted with the most extraordinary sight: Mrs Collins wearing an apron and cap, twirling round the room in a dance and smiling every time she caught her reflection in the mirror.

Ravi didn't come, he just called. Nani had picked up the phone.

'No, baba, there's no need for you to come now, we're all fine. Also I have a friend staying with me. Yes, quite right, it is nice company. And a help too.'

I dashed across the hall to get to the phone, determined to tell Ravi the truth about the dusty grey-brown stranger. But as I passed the kitchen I realised that Mrs Collins no longer looked dusty brown. In fact she looked really quite respectable. Nani, seeing me coming, had already put down the phone and wandered off.

'Ravi,' I hissed into the receiver. 'Come now. If you don't, then don't blame me.'

I could still hear Ravi laughing in my ear as I put down the phone. In the kitchen Nani and Mrs Collins were talking.

'You mustn't call me madam, Mrs Collins, it sounds so formal.'

'What shall I call you then? Mrs Datta?'

'You could call me by my name, Chand. It means moon.'

'Now what would I call you if we was in India?'

'In India? You'd probably call me Chandji. *Ji* means respected and we always add that on.'

'Chandji. I'll call you that then. And you must call me Edna.'

'Ednaji.'

Wasn't it all just so sweet and cosy. I resolved that if nobody else was worrying then neither would I. Once again we all settled into our routines. Mrs Collins took over two shelves in the hall cupboard, started putting her shoes next to ours on the shoe rack. She befriended both Cheryl and Annie, who would lap up her stories of upstairs and downstairs, sculleries, cauldrons of clothes and shining silver.

'In one place, Jewish bankers they were, they had so much silver that it took the whole Friday to polish it all.

We could only work as long as there was daylight y'see, because after that everything had to be shut down for the sabbath and we went off duty.'

Mrs Collins started to accompany Nani to jumble sales; they picked up an old sewing-machine and she then got busy transforming old clothes into smart outfits for herself. She also started to buy *The Lady* to 'look for a position as housekeeper companion'. Nani encouraged her, and by the time Ravi came up to visit, she really was both presentable and companionable. Ravi was quite taken by her, she called him 'Master Ravi', enquired about his studies, told him how she'd heard lots about him from Nani.

Mrs Collins even started to keep the fast with my grandmother, and one day I overheard her telling Cheryl that Nani didn't like it that my friends shortened my name, Divya, to Dee and Div.

'They don't mean anything, you see. But Divya has a meaning, it means divine. And they believe, you see, that words and names have energy. And she chose that name for her, you see.'

And then there was that time when Simon came. Simon was a friend of Ravi's. He arrived early and Mrs Collins let him in. I heard them talking in the sitting-room; Mrs Collins appeared to be telling him the story of Durga, who she was, why she rode a tiger and the meaning of all the weapons in her arms.

'Hello, Divya, you didn't know I knew all that, did you, dearie?' She smiled at me as I came in.

'Hello, Div,' smiled Simon. 'Do you know all these wonderful stories?'

'Chandji, the mistress that is, is a wonderful storyteller. But I must tell you truthfully that I was a bit frightened of all these when I first saw them until I found out that they're all stories and ideas really.'

Maybe I felt a bit jealous. I hadn't listened to Nani's stories for years and my mother and father were always too busy. And now she'd been telling them all to Mrs Collins. That night it was I who couldn't sleep and got up to creep around the house. Mrs Collins remained fast asleep.

It was the following Friday and I came home early and caught Mrs Collins rummaging through Nani's bag in the hall. She hadn't heard me open the front door as the kettle had just started to whistle. But when I came into the kitchen she looked startled.

'Your gran's not feeling too good.' Her tone seemed unsure. 'She had a dizzy spell, so I'm making her a hot drink.'

That night after a long time I once more heard the floorboards creak and the doors squeak. Mrs Collins was again prowling around.

The next day, Nani came into my room early to ask if she could borrow some money as she had mislaid her purse.

'I had a fall when I went out yesterday,' she said. 'On my way to the bank.'

The image of Mrs Collins and the bag flashed through my mind. 'How much did you have in it?'

'A hundred and fifty pounds. I'd just got it from the bank. I had a fall. I must have dropped it somewhere.' Nani was trying to remember.

Of course, I knew better. 'Did you say you fell on your way to the bank?'

'Someone once told me,' continued Nani, 'that if you turn a glass upside down and ask St Anthony to help, then whatever you've lost will be found. We can try it now, shall we?'

And if it's not lost, but stolen, will St Anthony catch the thief, or maybe even the thief repent, I said to myself as I went to the kitchen to get a glass.

Mrs Collins was sitting in her sunny spot reading *The Lady*, and marking things up as she went along. Butter would definitely not melt in her mouth, I said to myself.

She looked up at me. 'Everything all right?' she asked. So innocent! It was unbelievable. I started to wonder how many other things she had stolen during all the weeks she had had free rein of the house. I wrestled with the idea of confronting her there and then but my throat felt blocked. I walked out with the empty glass. Maybe St Anthony would sort it all out.

Later, I called Annie and told her about Nani having lost her purse. I told her how upset Nani was, which wasn't true. I knew Mrs Collins could overhear.

'Was there money in the purse your gran lost?' Mrs Collins asked when I came back into the kitchen.

'Of course there was. She'd just been to the bank, hadn't she!'

Mrs Collins closed her magazine and looked uncomfortable. And so she should, I thought. Maybe I also thought I was giving St Anthony a helping hand.

The next morning Nani came into my room looking fragile and bewildered. 'Ednaji is not there. She has taken all her things and gone. Did she say anything to you?'

I was taken aback but pretended otherwise. 'Nani, can't you see that she's just stolen your money and left.'

'But she didn't need to do that, Divya. She could have just asked me, she knew that.'

'Well, she was not what she seemed,' I said with great certainty. 'I warned you at the very beginning.'

'Did you say something to her, Divya?' Nani's voice was very gentle.

'No. I just told Annie. She heard me and realised her game was up and left. It's so obvious, can't you see?'

Nani just nodded absently.

It was early Monday morning that the bank called. I was getting late for school, but I picked up the phone. They had found Nani's purse. She'd dropped it there. There was money in it and would she like to come and identify it.

I didn't go to school that day, or the next. I went instead to Victoria station and wandered around through the lockers, the benches, the ladies, the platforms, the cafés. Then I wrote out an advertisement for *The Lady*.

'Mrs Collins, Ednaji. Please come back. Forgive me. Divya.'

I was crying, so I didn't hear Nani as she slipped into my room, but was soothed by the lilt of her voice. It was her special storytelling voice.

'Life is full of lessons. And there is always more to learn.' I swallowed my tears and held my breath. 'Long time ago now, when the partition riots were going on and we were trying to make our way out of Lahore, to the new Indian border, I got separated from my family and couldn't find them anywhere. I was very frightened. I was only twenty and it was such a terrible, terrible time. Everything seemed to be on fire, and the air was thick with smoke and hate.

'A Muslim family who had themselves just escaped from India and lost their own daughter on the way, took pity and adopted me. They called me Rashida. They protected me, and in spite of all their sorrow, and at great risk to themselves, they eventually got me to safety. I vowed never to forget, never. As it was Ekadashi I decided to keep the fast in memory.'

The Ekadashi fast is reputed to develop inner strength and wisdom. I've kept it for seven years now and the lessons of that time continue to unfold.

We never did hear from Ednaji again, and I still read the personal column in *The Lady*. But since that summer I have never been the same. I grew up then, and sometimes, I wonder if Mrs Collins appeared just for that to happen.

Fifty-Fifty Tutti-Frutti Chocolate-Chip
Norman Silver

Norman Silver was born in South Africa and now lives in Suffolk, England. He spent time working in remand homes for teenagers in London and Bristol and is now a full-time writer for young people. This story is told by a white boy, who witnesses the violence and racism of the apartheid regime in South Africa. It describes how his own ideals and beliefs are affected by the system that surrounds him.

As you read, *think about the character of the narrator, Basil. The story is written in the first person to allow us to identify with him and understand his thoughts. How far do you see him as a typical teenager, and where do you find yourself disagreeing with his beliefs and actions?*

I'm sure the nicest ice-cream in the whole world comes from Napoli. If you're ever in Sea Point you must try it. They do a fifty-fifty tutti-frutti chocolate-chip with almond topping that does full justice to God's creation of a tongue. Somehow that particular ice-cream sets off every taste-bud on your tongue with a rhythm of sensations that you won't get anywhere else, I'm sure of it.

That Napoli restaurant won't mind me advertising them, because for a month, while I was holidaying at my grandparents' flat in Sea Point, I was a regular customer there. Every night, about half-past eleven, I'd arrive there for my treat. After the first week, I didn't even have to say what I wanted.

'Good evening, sir. Two fifty-fifty tutti-frutti chocolate-chips with almond topping?'

After that, the walk from Napoli to Green Point was delicious, with this ice-cream cone in my hand, and the taste-bud music popping on my tongue.

Of course, holding hands with Sandra while we walked was nice, too. Especially as she had this neat habit of softly rubbing the palm of my hand with her thumb.

Mind you, I've always fancied ice-creams. When I was a kid my dad and ma used to take me out on these weekend picnics, to Hout Bay or Camps Bay, or the Strand, or Stellenbosch, or Paarl. We would drive for miles to find the right place to picnic. I didn't mind a bit, because I knew they'd buy me a rainbow ice-cream when we stopped.

My dad and ma used to sing all these songs as we drove along like 'Row, row, row your boat, gently down the stream, merrily, merrily, merrily, merrily, life is but a dream'. However, the dream had begun long ago to fade into reality as my parents and me clashed more and more about everything, and in particular about choosing a decent career for myself.

I've always been interested in journalism, but my dad and ma had other ideas. On my fourteenth birthday they surprised me with this present of a book called *The Miracle of the Human Body*. It came complete with colourful transparencies, so that across the white bones of the skeleton you could overlay pictures of the muscles, or the blood vessels, or the vital organs, or the nervous system, etc., etc.

I couldn't see myself why this book should have any interest for me, particularly as seeing blood wasn't my speciality, but the inscription on the inside cover made it perfectly clear: 'To our dear son Basil, the future doctor (or surgeon, or specialist), may this book help you on your way to a dedicated career devoted to helping others, from Popidoo and Momidoo.'

That was a monumental day in my life, because not only was the book heavy as hell, but I could feel the pressure from my parents was also as heavy as hell.

For a while I tried every possible tactic to accidentally destroy this book and my parents' plans for my future. I dumped it in the garbage bin by accident; I put it in a cardboard box of clothes which my mother was giving to charity. But the book was miraculous in more than just name. Each time it returned from the dead.

Once I even took it with me on a weekend to relations in Mossel Bay and accidentally left it behind when we returned to Cape Town. But a month later it arrived, wrapped in brown paper, with a note from my aunt explaining that her servant girl, Eileen, had found it stuck behind the wardrobe in the room where I had slept. She felt obliged to post it back to me because she knew how much I must be missing it.

In the end I decided to ceremonially burn the book one afternoon in our **braaivleis** in the backyard. (My dad made that braaivleis from a metal barrel, which he found somewhere; he sawed it in half and attached a wire grille across the open hole.) I can tell you that it took a lot of guts to burn that book on the altar which my dad had constructed with his own hands. As the flames leapt into action, doing their mysterious dance of death on each of the one thousand three hundred and eighty-nine curling pages of that book, my heart

---

braaivleis: barbecue

also was doing its mysterious dance of breaking free from my parents' control.

When it came to Sunday lunch-time and my dad began to prepare the fire, a half-burnt image of the large intestines stared up at him from the ashes in the bottom of the barrel. You could clearly read that it was page 743, but even so, I was surprised that my dad made the connection as quickly as he did. After all, how could he have guessed my murderous intentions towards that book? He was furious.

'That book cost fifty-something **rands**! You've burnt to ashes a good career.'

Thereafter, steaks grilled on that braai didn't taste so good; it was as if the burnt picture of the large intestines hovered like a ghoul at the spot where the book had been sacrificed.

But I needed to make that statement about the direction of my own life. That was also the reason why I chose to go on holiday on my own to Sea Point that summer. I know it wasn't much of a distance from our house in Claremont to Sea Point – it was only two bus rides away – but at least it was one means of getting a break from my parents' nagging. For a while they tried to force me to take my young brother Ivan with me. That would have spoiled everything! Imagine having to drag around a nine-year-old wherever I went!

No, my parents would have to get used to the idea that I was an independent person and almost an adult. And when I met Sandra on that holiday, I reckoned my folks would also have to get used to the idea that I was

---

rands: South African money

capable of having a serious and mature relationship with a girl.

When I used to drop Sandra off at her house in Green Point, I would give her a final goodnight kiss tasting of fifty-fifty tutti-frutti chocolate-chip Napoli ice-cream, and arrange to meet her the next day.

Then I'd run all the way back to my grandparents' flat in Sea Point. Actually it wasn't real running. It was more like what you do in some dreams, when you suddenly find that if you tilt your body horizontal to the ground, you are able to fly just by small movements of your hands. It was a sensational feeling! My running steps each seemed to take me about five metres, and I felt so light as I ran along the seafront like that, hardly noticing any of the people who were still promenading up and down in the moonlight.

I suppose I still couldn't believe that Sandra actually liked me so much, and was making herself so available to me, with her deep kisses and intimate cuddles. After all, she was a good looker.

Of course, being after midnight, it was mostly couples promenading, and doing a few other things, too, in the shadows or behind walls. In the daytime and early evening, the seafront belonged to the crowds of old folks and families. And my grandparents were among them.

Everyone knew my grandparents. You could tell them a mile off by the way they walked, with my grandmother leaning heavily on my grandfather's shoulder, and dragging her stiff, artificial leg along as best she could. It never bent properly, that was the problem, and it took her ages to sit down on a bench to rest. So many people stopped to talk to her; everyone loved her, I think, with her warm personality. And although my grandfather maintained that the amputation of her leg had been unnecessary, a medical error of some sort, my grandmother always said she was grateful at least to be mobile. There were so many people, she said, who were too ill or handicapped to be able to enjoy the pleasure of the seafront. (But to tell the truth, in the privacy of her own flat, I used to see her crying sometimes, feeling sorry for herself. Who could blame her, though?)

Most of the summer the seafront had a leisurely, holiday atmosphere. But every New Year the place went wild, especially at night. Local residents had made complaints every year to the police, but still nothing had been done to prevent drunk revellers from rampaging through the streets and kicking up a rumpus right through till the early hours of morning.

Sandra and me spent a quiet New Year's Day together alone on a crowded beach, sharing our affections and resolutions. One of the things I resolved was to pursue the career of journalism in the face of all opposition.

It wasn't only my parents who felt I should not be a journalist. This one teacher, Bonzo, gave us hundreds of aptitude tests and guess what conclusion he came to? He came up with this brilliant suggestion of me taking up accountancy. Me! Such a sensitive person with insight into the human condition! Me! An accountant? I told old Bonzo that he didn't know his arse from his elbow.

This assessment of his ability didn't go down too well, and he gave me the option of rubber tyre or cricket bat.

Bonzo was into violence in a big way. He had this mildly annoying habit of walking around the classroom while we were all concentrating on filling in questionnaires or something. The room would be deadly quiet, but then, with an amused smile on his lips, he would raise his hand to shoulder height and bring it down with full force on some unsuspecting back. The surprise alone, never mind the searing pain, could have killed a boy with a weak heart, but fortunately there weren't any in our class. The handprint would remain on the victim's back for several hours afterwards.

He also had a collection of weapons in the storeroom behind the class which he used with regularity to educate our backsides. There were a dozen canes of varying thicknesses and lengths, cricket bats, tennis rackets, hockey sticks, rubber hoses, pieces of rubber tyre nailed to handles, ropes, lengths of electric cord, and, of course, planks of varying thicknesses and suppleness. I personally think he chose the wrong career for himself: instead of being a teacher at a crappy Cape Town high school, he should have entered the police force.

With regard to the punishment, I was lucky. Although the rubber tyre had a painful reputation, the cricket bat was known as one of the softer options. Also, it was a well-established fact that every night Bonzo looked too deep in the bottle, and therefore he didn't use as much force in the mornings, because he didn't like to jolt his hangovered head.

In spite of that, the beating put me right off choosing any career, and I decided to look into the possibilities of becoming a professional surf-bum.

However, that was just an idle fantasy: for one thing, I didn't know how to use a surfboard; for another, my skin tends to go a painful red in the sun.

But it was worth the sunburn, sitting there the whole day on the beach with Sandra, only occasionally getting up to swim in the breakers or to play beach tennis with each other. We made a wonderful twosome.

We used to spend most evenings in Sea Point. And this one particular evening after New Year, wherever we walked there were all these coloured **Coons** (or are we supposed to call them Minstrels nowadays?), left over from the day's Carnival, hanging round in twos and threes, dressed up in their satiny costumes, all turquoise and pink and brown and white and green and yellow, playing their lively tambourines and banjos and saxophones and singing '**Dis die Nuwejaar en ons is bymekaar, Bokkie jy moet huis toe gaan**.'

I liked the look of those Coons. Their colours were just like the colours of the fifty-fifty tutti-frutti chocolate-chip Napoli ice-creams that were dripping over our hands as we licked them and listened to the music. When they held out their satiny hats, I gave them a few coins for singing and harmonising so well.

It was easily worth the money, because on the way back to Green Point that night, Sandra and I sang their song that it was the New Year and we were together and it was time for Bokkie to go home. After that I called Sandra 'Bokkie' for the rest of the month.

Then I did my usual flying-running past the seafront on my way home.

Coons: participants in the Cape Carnival (formerly the Coon Carnival)

'**Dis die Nuwejaar . . .**': 'It is the New Year and we are together, Bokkie you must go home.'

But that night I had to crash-land suddenly, because there was a hell of a fight going on. I must have had my head so brightly lit with the memory of Sandra's cuddliness that I forgot to avoid the seafront which I should have known would be wild.

These five white blokes were beating up these two Coons. One white bloke was using a banjo as a lethal weapon, striking the Coons repeatedly with it, and yelling 'Hey darling! Here you are darling!' with each blow he struck.

A group of white girls were huddled by this one bench, drinking out of beer bottles, watching the fight and apparently giggling.

I tell you, those white blokes were cross about something. They kept kicking the Coons in their guts and in their backsides and any other part of their bodies that lay open to attack.

'You don't ever call a white chick "Darling". **Verstaan!** I don't care if it's bladdy New Year. You stick to your own kind!'

Eventually, when their violence blew out like a candle, they rejoined the girls and stood round for a while drinking and throwing their empty bottles on to the outcrops of rocks. One of the blokes urinated at the side of the pavement before they all continued their promenading up the beach, with their arms around the tight-jeaned backsides of the girls. The tallest chap thumped the roof of every parked car he passed with his heavy fist. I'm sure their owners must have been very overjoyed in the morning to find their cars suffering from hangovers.

Verstaan!: Understand!

The banjo had been thrown on to the beach sand and it lay there like a monument, gleaming in the broken moonlight.

I remember when I used to go fishing with my dad on rocky outcrops, I used to find these shattered pieces of bottle glass lying everywhere and I always used to wonder who filthed those places. Now I knew!

Violence has always upset me a lot, but as I stood there keeping my distance and deciding what to do, it occurred to me that what I had just witnessed should be turned into a penetrating article for a newspaper or a magazine.

I had to do something. I walked on to the soft sand and picked up the banjo. Its white circular skin was torn, and some strings were broken. The metal bits were also bent and dented, and the long arm that sticks out was deformed. It was one hell of a mess.

I took it across to the two Coons. They were even more torn and broken and bent and dented than the banjo, I think. Blood was running out of the one man's nose, and his hair was also matted with blood. I could hardly look at him, though I wished I could help him.

'Eina! Eina! Ag, Ma, ek'seer!'

He kept calling for his ma, and rubbing his bloody head with his hand. But at least he was going to survive. It was the other bloke who looked really bad. I couldn't see much blood on him, but he was just lying there immobilised on the concrete; the shape of his body didn't look too good.

'Here's your banjo,' I said to the one who was moaning. 'It's broken but maybe you can get it fixed.'

'But how can *I* get fixed?' he asked me. 'My life pains me too much.'

I felt terrible standing there. I wanted to do something. I wanted, at least, to tell that at that moment I wasn't too proud of being white.

There are some things you can never say. I remember when those weekend drives we used to go on turned into arguments between my ma and dad, about where to picnic, and most of the journey would be spent on arguing. Then a gloom would set in, and the journey would be silent for hour after hour, and they wouldn't find a picnic place that suited both of them. I sat in the back of that car and somehow I knew that I couldn't say anything to my parents.

I felt like screaming for them to stop, but I sat in silence. Eventually they'd stop somewhere and buy me a rainbow ice-cream to make *me* feel better at least, but they would just continue their arguing.

I couldn't think of anything to say to that injured coloured, so I just tried to help him get up. Leaning on me, he managed to drag himself to the bench. The second coloured was lights out.

'You guys stay here!' I said to the one on the bench, though I don't how I expected either of them to move in their condition. 'I'll go and get help for you.'

As I ran the few blocks to my grandparents' flat, I began to shape in my head the article I would write about racial violence. The thought of becoming a journalist exhilarated me. If only I could persuade my parents. But then I remembered the look of shock on my ma's face, the time I told her that I was considering taking up journalism.

'Go ahead and do whatever you want,' she generously said. 'It's your decision. If you're not interested in

Medical School, what does my opinion matter? I'm only your mother.'

My dad had been equally generous.

'So be a reporter for some lousy newspaper! You'll either end up a poor white, or you'll end up in prison.'

I was pleased one day, though, when my dad met a bloke who was a journalist, albeit for the *Farmer's Weekly* or some other **japie** magazine. Their antagonism towards my choice of career was slightly lessened when this fellow explained that the money wasn't too bad if you got a good training and made the right contacts.

But I'll tell you the truth: money never meant that much to me. We used to have this board game called Careers, in which you have to choose a certain proportion of three things and then achieve it in your lifetime. The three things were money, fame and happiness. I was such a sucker at the time (can you believe it?) I used to opt for 100 per cent happiness. Nobody could win playing the game that way, and of course now I'd go for a sensible mix of all three. People used to think I was such a sap choosing 100 per cent happiness, and it's probably not surprising that I never ever won a single game of Careers. That was in itself quite frustrating, because no one likes to play a game without ever winning, do they?

Quite recently I met this girl Janine, and she told me that she divides the world into winners and losers and that she only goes out with blokes who are winners. It's really odd, because even though I've changed a lot since I used to play Careers, she still wouldn't go out

---

japie: stupid

with me, even though *I* thought we'd get on like a house on fire.

I was out of breath when I reached the flat. I quietly let myself in with the key. My grandparents were both asleep but woke when they heard me phoning for an ambulance.

'Are you all right, Basil?' my grandmother shouted out from her bed. 'Who needs an ambulance? Is Sandra hurt, God forbid?'

I went into their bedroom to reassure them that Sandra and me were both okay. Their room had a smell of old people, slightly medicinal, and my grandmother's artificial leg stood in its shoe leaning up against a chair near her bed.

'There's two blokes hurt on the promenade,' I said. 'They need to get to the hospital.'

'Don't go back there, Basil!' my grandmother said. 'You'll get into trouble. There's **meshugena** people out there.'

'It's all right,' I said. 'I'll only be five minutes.'

I ran out of the flat and down to the bench on the seafront, but the two injured Coons were nowhere to be seen. I knew I was at the right place because of the bench and because the puddle of urine was still there at the side of the pavement. But there was no signs of the Coons! Even the damaged banjo had been taken off somewhere.

The next day, when I told Sandra what had happened, she said those coloureds were probably looking for trouble and that's why they got beaten up.

'Hey, Bokkie! Don't say such things!'

---

meshugena: crazy

The rest of my holiday, Sandra and me tried to get really close to each other. My grandmother made the best picnic lunches ever – like cold chicken, **potato latkes** and water-melon – and Sandra and me spent the long sun-drenched days in each other's company, enjoying the beach and the waves and each other's fondness.

But in the last week we started arguing about where to go for our picnics, and she said she had never been too fond of fifty-fifty tutti-frutti chocolate-chip Napoli ice-creams, and that it was much better to keep the flavours separate. (She also mentioned that my squint got on her nerves.) I decided then to take Bokkie home for the last time, and I never saw her again.

Later, I did send my article about the beating up of the Coons to a newspaper, but they didn't accept it. It was returned with a brief note explaining that if I ever came across a newsworthy story I should contact the paper so that one of their reporters could come round to get the details.

Since then I've gone off journalism. It strikes me as something for which you really need dedication. It is something you have to be prepared to go to prison for. And I don't really know if I've got those sorts of ideals.

So what am I going to do instead for a career? My final choice seemed so natural in the end, so right, so easy, as if I'd been destined all along to make this decision.

I'll give you a moment to guess what I'm going to do. I only decided quite recently.

I think it's the perfect choice.

I have decided to go to Medical School.

---

potato latkes: potato cakes

That's right, I've decided I want to be a doctor. And not just an ordinary doctor. No, I intend to specialise in psychiatry, because I feel I have a lot of insight into how people's minds work. I can see through hypocrisy and the games people play and get right down to the very centre of what makes people tick.

So in a few years time, you'll see me qualifying as a psychiatrist, just you wait. And that surely proves the inaccuracy of Bonzo's aptitude tests, and at the same time it proves the wisdom and foresight of parents, doesn't it? They always knew I'd be a doctor. I tell you, they were so over the moon, they promised they'd buy me a car at the end of my first year at Medical School.

I am convinced a medical career is the perfect choice for me. I always wanted to dedicate and devote myself to other people. And if I make money in the process and become wealthy and famous, well, that's part of winning the Careers game, isn't it?

Two Kinda Truth
Farrukh Dhondy

This story is set in modern Britain and addresses a range of cultures that a boy experiences in his school and social life. Farrukh Dhondy describes modern cultures such as the black rap and music scenes, and how these relate to what a teenager might experience in school. Bonny is a poet, but his English teacher questions how far his rapping and ranting are really poetry.

As you read, *think about the character of Bonny. Do you admire him and, if so, why? What are the reasons for his difficult behaviour in school?*

My name is Irving, but they call me Clyde on account of my friend Bonny. Bonny and I used to go together from the time we knew almost nothing. You could say we grew together. We went to the same primary school and then to the same big school and we always met after, and on Saturdays we washed cars down the street together and split the **breads** we made from that and from anything else. We weren't like twins, because I was like Bonny's shadow. I even caught my name off him. The youth then, they started to call us **Bonny and Clyde** after we were accused of doing the same robbery. The name stuck, even though the charge of robbery didn't. We got off because this smart lawyer . . . but that's another story, yes?

breads: money
Bonny and Clyde: famous American criminals in the 1930s

Bonny, boy, he grew smarter than any of the youth we used to hang around with. The first day we moved to this dread school in Battersea, he takes one look around the place and says, 'It soft. Man could be happy here.' Now, looking back on it, I don't know how we could have made such a mistake. That school was split up in three. There was the main building, all new and still being built, where they kept the smart ones. They were all white and one or two Asian kids and a couple of blacks. We were kept in what we called the 'coal heap'. It was down in Wandsworth and we called it that because there was a whole heap of coal in the yard. The teachers, they called it the 'Annexe'. There was only a few whites up there, most of the youths on the heap was black.

We stayed in that place three years before we was moved and had to come up to the main building because it was complete and the heap was shut forever. Before that we only saw the main building when the coaches fetched us to carol services or some other jive occasion and the headmaster would stand up and do he thing.

Anyway, this story's not about that school and about blacks and whites, because it would have to be longer than the longest book anybody so far writ. This story's about Wordsy and Bonny. Wordsy was a teacher. He wasn't called 'Wordsy' at all – that was the name Bonny gave him. He was an English teacher. No, first he was a student guy, one of the people who come and waste your time because they're training to be teachers and they need guinea-pigs. We met him, all those years ago, in our English class. Old man Cottage usually came in and gave us some spelling test or told us to read 'The

English Way Reader, Book I, II or III'. But this day here, Wordsy come through the door. He was carrying a handbag on his shoulder. He was a young guy with long hair, kinda hippy. He walk in cool, cool, and say to us that Mr Cottage was going to come down and introduce him, but he was a man believe in his own introduction.

Most of the youth just mucked about in that place. We never listened to nobody. We just didn't want to know. When we got to know Wordsy, years later, he told us that he was nervous that first time, like really shaking. He'd never been in a class before and he was not even sure that he should have been teaching. And we told him that he shouldn't have brought his handbag with him. He should've suss the place and come with a briefcase or something.

As soon as the youth saw the handbag they began to shout 'butty, butty, **butty man**'. Of course Wordsy didn't twig what they were calling him. He wanted some quiet, so he rapped on the teacher's desk and stood up straight to show that we couldn't mess with him. But nobody would listen. It was like that; we always tested out the newcomers. Then Wordsy tried getting hold of one of the youth in the front and tried to reason with him.

Bonny just watched him careful. Then he said, '**Hush your clamour** and let the man speak.' That's how Bonny talked, always a bit fancy. They called him a wordsman. Immediately, Wordsy saw that Bonny was some kinda leader in that mob, so he turned to him.

---

butty man: a reference to homosexuality
Hush your clamour: Shut up

Then Bonny stood up and turned to the class and started bowing and making a little speech and everyone turned to watch him and laugh. He pretended he was mucking about, but really he was getting everyone's attention, helping Wordsy along.

'All right, now that you're quiet, we can start,' Wordsy said, but even Bonny's effect didn't last long and the others started throwing things at the man. He just sink down in the teacher's chair and say he'll sit there till it quiet.

'You'll have to be bury in that chair, sir,' Bonny said. 'It never going to be quiet, we ain't quiet for nobody.'

As the class went on Wordsy got desperate. He'd brought some papers along and me and Bonny walked up to his desk and asked him what he'd got there. He showed us. It was some poem by a man called Wordsworth and Bonny asked him if he'd writ it himself. The man say that he wish all his life he had writ it, but he hadn't.

'You got the copyright, then?' Bonny asked, just to be feisty. Then he shouted to the class that the man was called Wordsworth and he was no ordinary man here, he was a PO-YET. The class wasn't interested. Bonny looked at the sheet and said, 'Hmm, it all right,' and Wordsy smiled, but he was nearly crying before the bell went and he'd wasted the whole lesson.

Two days later, when we'd all forgotten the guy, he comes back. English was in the afternoon and it was in a classroom just by this heap of coal, looking out on the yard. The room had huge windows, like doors almost. When he come in, the whole class cheered.

Bonny nudged me with his elbow because he had a key to the doors of all the rooms in that place and he indicated to me that we should lock the door so that Wordsy wouldn't be able to get out. The man was trying to smile. In the confusion, Bonny slipped over to the door and locked it up.

'You see I haven't given up with you,' Wordsy told the class.

'What's your name?' they were asking.

'Never mind my name. Let's get down to some reading,' he said and he distributed the papers straight away. He began to read as soon as the papers had reached our desks.

'"Let us go then, you and I,"' he read.

'I ain't going nowhere with you,' someone shouted.

'Are you really a butty, sir?'

'This man drunk,' one of the boys in the front row shouted.

'To tell you the truth,' Wordsy said, 'to face you lot, one has to be either drunk or superhuman or mad. And since I can't induce the **oblivion** of madness, and since God made me painfully mortal, I've had what we call a little nip, as weakness shall be my witness.'

'Your breath smell foul, sir,' the boy in the front said.

'Talk fancy again,' Bonny said. 'This guy's good, you's a preacher man like old Cottage.'

Bonny always appreciated that sort of style. Cottage would talk a bit like the Bible, you know, a bit of high talk. 'Do unto thy brethren as they would do unto you. Betray them. Grass them up,' he'd say, and then he'd say, 'Put your hands on your hearts, remember your **Maker**

---

oblivion: forgetfulness
Maker: God

and confess to throwing chunks of coal through the staff-room window, or I'll flog the lot of you.'

The youth liked that. Cottage kept order with the cane, and with little tricks like that. He'd talk grand and then he'd talk cockney all of a sudden and it make everyone laugh, but it make them scared at the same time.

Wordsy read his poem after that, and he got the hiccups and some boys rushed over and started hitting him on the back, saying they'd make his hiccups go away. By the time the lesson was finished, Bonny was saying to me, 'This man all right.' I could see that Bonny liked the way he was talking, using big words, laying it on when he found the class silent for a moment. Bonny was fascinated by words even then. If we went to a blues, he'd listen to the new lyrics and dub tunes and try and learn the rough bits and change them here and there and use them himself in his speech.

By the time the bell went the youth were waiting to see how Wordsy would get out of the room. They all knew the door was locked. He tried the door. Then the boys crowded round him and asked him if they could see his handbag, and if he had a boy-friend and all kind of rudeness. Wordsy was desperate to get out. He crossed over to the big windows and tried to open one. It was jammed shut. The schoolkeeper had nailed it down to keep kids from running out of that classroom. Wordsy didn't see the nails and he just banged on the catch harder and harder till he missed, and his fist went clean through the window, smashing the glass.

'That's school property,' someone shouted.

It wasn't a joke. The glass had cut right through Wordsy's wrist and the blood was pouring out. Wordsy fell to the floor saying, 'Oh my God,' and holding his wrist, his eyes wide with disbelief.

Bonny pushed the others aside and went up and knelt by him. There was going to be trouble now, we could all smell it. The joke had gone too far.

'Go sit down,' Bonny motioned to the rest and they did as he said.

'Mr Wordsworth,' Bonny said and the student man looked up. There were tears in his eyes and still the blood flowed. 'Shall I call Mr Cottage?'

The man shook his head. The class was dead silent now.

'Gimme hanky,' Bonny shouted.

Someone gave him a coloured hanky and he tied it round the man's wrist. Wordsy looked finished, boy, he couldn't even kneel straight, he was going to topple over.

'Go get Cottage,' Bonny said to me, holding the man upright.

'Mr Wordsworth, hang on there, guy, we fetching somebody.'

Wordsy shook his head.

'My breath,' he said, 'drink. Don't call Cottage.'

Bonny understood. He got the key out of his desk and rushed up to the staff room to call the young drama teacher. He was thinking right. She was also a bit hip, like Wordsy, and she wouldn't grass him up. She came down and took him away.

We didn't see Wordsy again till we'd nearly finished with the main school. I was in the sixth form. Bonny left at the end of the fifth, telling the head that he wanted to look a job. He didn't look a work. He just came back when he got fed up of lounging about and told the sixth-year master that he had been discriminated against and all the jobs always went to the white boys and all this, and they sympathised with him and let him back into the sixth form, even though he hadn't been bothered to take any CSE or O levels or nothing.

Bonny told the head that he was interested in maths because he could get some technical training after, but we knew that he wasn't really. He was just interested in relax. He joined the English class because I was there. I'd done my O levels and I was going on to do A level English. I was interested in it. I liked reading books. When Wordsy reappeared and started doing his kind of thing, English became more interesting. In a way even Bonny admitted that Wordsy was good.

Wordsy came back as a teacher this time. He didn't look much older to us.

'Where did I check you before?' Bonny said, strolling up to him in the sixth-form room. 'I see you before somewhere, Jah.'

'You tell me,' Wordsy said.

'You was a bouncer in the Stalawart Club up in Islington, right?' Bonny grinned, 'and you call **the Babylon** when things get too hot for yuh to handle, right? And the youth swore revenge as they drag him off to prison to do some heavy pieces. But now I break loose of the dread **calaboose** and I come for my revenge.' Bonny stretched two fingers out in a mock gun.

---

the Babylon: the police
calaboose: jail

Wordsy caught on fast. He raised his hands and said, 'You may have shot the Sheriff, but you mustn't shoot the deputy.'

'Nice, nice, nice,' Bonny said, 'you all right?'

'Have I seen you before?' Wordsy asked, narrowing his eyes.

'You still owe me one hanky, for bandage your hand,' Bonny reminded him.

'Of course,' Wordsy said with real wonder and astonishment and respect, 'of course. You know when I came in this morning I asked some of the staff if the old three-ten were still around and they said, "Yes, some of them." What they meant really was, "God send the plagues to try us instead of these pupils." How are you?'

Bonny was never in Wordsy's class, but Wordsy would let him come and sit in on lessons.

'Not for the work,' Bonny would say, 'I like being with my *spa* Clyde.' But Wordsy could see that when we were discussing poetry or reading it in class, Bonny's attention was just there. Bonny and I had never split up really. Even during the term he was off school and I was doing exams, I'd see him a few evenings a week. He began to move with a new crowd but I tagged along with them and we went to the 'Centre' in the evenings. A whole **posse** of youth hung out there. It was supposed to be a youth club, so two nights a week there were sounds, and sometimes guys hired the place and brought in Coxson and Sofrano B and the big boys. The rest of the time, the Centre was

---

spa: mate
posse: gang

boredom and hustle. Guys would sell weed and just use it as a meeting place for play ping-pong and dominoes, and drift in and out of the Judo class which was run twice a week by a Japanese man.

Though Bonny had made some kind of mark, even there, he was just a swordfish with a lot of sharks around. Maybe that was why he wanted to come back to school. He'd got some sort of reputation as a dread man. Not that Bonny is heavy or heavy-looking. He's thin as a whip, but fast, you know, real fast. And he could talk. He'd got in with a gang of youth who ran a sound system called 'Kool Skank', and when they were playing at the Centre, Bonny would take the mike and play DJ. He'd carry on a whole rap in front of the music, imitating Big Youth and Jah Stitch and Dr Almantado. He was building himself a small reputation as a real dub artist, a man whose toasting was really hot.

That was the time Wordsy started his poetry circle. He'd done some writing himself and he always boasted that he had friends who'd written real books and poems. I said I was interested and so did Bonny. On Wednesday nights we'd stay after school, and several

girls from the English set would stay behind too and Wordsy would give us some sherry to drink and we'd go up the staff room when nobody was there and start the sessions with him reading some poetry. That was his little trip. He'd read some T.S. Eliot and then some guy called Hopkins which was like Rasta poetry about God and thing. Bonny said, 'They all sound like West Indians, them poets, with names like **Gerard** and **Wystan** and **Dylan**.'

He'd ask Wordsy some funny questions, but really honest. He would ask, 'How man could learn hard words?' or he'd ask, 'Could you lend me a book with all the rhyming words in English inside?'

Wordsy didn't like them kind of questions, but he'd try and answer them serious.

'Don't obsess yourself with impressing people,' he'd say. 'A poem doesn't have to rhyme. Rhyme is a sort of escapism.'

'Rhyme is musi-kal,' Bonny would reply.

'Well, it depends,' Wordsy would argue. 'A poem has to have its own internal music, something more convincing than rhyme.' Then he'd leaf through the books piled by his chair and say, 'You hear that? It seems to have the whole rhythm of speech.'

'I ain't speak like that,' Bonny would say, 'You don't speak like that either. Find me a man who talk so. Poetry is not natural talk. If you talk like that on the street man will think you mad.'

Wordsy would fend off the arguments. 'You have to be a little mad to write with inspiration. Poets,

---

Gerard, **Wystan**, **Dylan**: the poets G.M. Hopkins, W.H. Auden and Dylan Thomas drunkards, madmen, you know what Shakespeare said about lovers . . .'

Bonny was impatient with Shakespeare. He'd ask if Wordsy had managed to sell any of his poems. The others would get shifty, and yet they enjoyed the sort of interruptions that Bonny would offer.

Wordsy would say no, he hadn't sold none, but success was a bitch goddess, it was not what a poet should be after. A poet should work like a carpenter, finding the right-sized nail, shaping the right joints between his thoughts.

'And between him fingers,' Bonny would say, 'are true, are true, are true. You sight it?'

Wordsy's stuff made some sense to me because you have to learn all that to get through A level, but Bonny said it made no sense to him, it was all failure-talk. Sometimes the girls would bring their poems and read them aloud to the circle. Wordsy would sit back, biting his lip and pretending to think hard about the words. Bonny would watch him. The poems were all about high-rise flats and how depressing they were and about loneliness and old people on park benches and shit.

'Methers again,' Bonny would say and look at me.

One day Bonny brought his own poems. He'd kept them a secret. Only now and then he dropped me a hint that he was going to be a great poet.

'Hold on there,' Bonny said as the session started. 'I and I have something here I want to present to the attention of this circle.'

Wordsy was pleased. He always wanted other people to read before he dragged out his own typed stuff.

Bonny took his floppy cap off and lifted the sheets from under it. The girls laughed.

'This one come straight out of my head,' he said. This was the poem:

All across the nation
Black man suffer aggravation
Babylon face us with iration
Man must reach some desperation.
It have to be iron, brothers y'all, it have to be iron,
   my sisters.

Babylon hold up the power
Black man reach the final hour
*Our strength in **Jah** is like a tower*
Bringing down a merciless shower
Of bitter rain, my brothers y'all, of bitter rain, my
   sisters.

He read the verses with tremendous seriousness. The others listened and, as he read, their eyes darted to Wordsy, who was sitting with his head in his hands and his elbows perched on his knees.

Bonny finished and met with absolute silence.

'What's wrong with it?' he asked aggressively.

'Oh, nothing, nothing in the least,' Wordsy said. 'It's fine, just one or two things, a couple of small points.'

The rest of us didn't say nothing. We were in Wordsy's English class and we knew that when he didn't approve of somebody's work he'd say, 'Fine, fine, a couple of points,' and then he'd launch in for the kill.

'Don't dig no horrors,' Bonny said. 'No big thing, say what you like.'

Jah: Jehovah, God

I knew that there was a certain amount of defiance in Bonny's voice. It was like an unsureness. He'd stuck his neck out and now he was going to protect it, but he had to know where the attack was coming from.

'I can, or at least I *think* I can, appreciate what you're trying to say.'

'Deaf don't even hear thunder,' Bonny said, quickly.

'Quite, quite,' Wordsy said, licking his lips which had gone dry. He was pulling some determination out of himself. 'Yet it seems like you've thrown together a lot of words without much thought.'

'I think all the time, you don't need a degree to think.'

'For God's sake, I'm not saying . . .' Wordsy trailed off. 'Well, all right, I'll give it to you straight. I think there's a lot of rhyme there, but there's no poetry, if you see what I mean. I don't mean to be discouraging, your sound patterns certainly show you've absorbed something, but there's no personal emotion. The poem is too much of a slogan; to be poetry it has to have the sound, not of **propaganda** but of, well, how shall I put it, of *truth*.'

Bonny screwed up his face. He put the poem back under his maroon velvet cap.

'Yeah?' he asked. He was hurt. He kissed his teeth.

'But we can ask the others. We should get more opinions,' Wordsy said. The girls were embarrassed, either by Bonny's righteous, strong poem, or by Wordsy's reaction.

'All right,' Bonny said. 'It cool. But remember,' and he got up to leave and turned round as he was

propaganda: information that promotes a particular point of view

leaving, 'remember, Mr Wordsworth, that there's *two* kinda truth.'

'There was no need for that,' Wordsy said after he'd gone. 'No need for anyone to take criticism so personally. If you're a writer, your work is public property, it's not your little toy . . .'

There were no more poetry sessions. The circle was closed.

Bonny didn't appear in the English lessons the next day. Then he dropped away from school. Wordsy seemed tense and nervous in those days. He never mentioned Bonny to me and he stopped calling me Clyde. He started calling me 'Irving' and I stopped calling him 'Mr Wordsworth'. Bonny disappeared from school. Once, when the sixth-form master asked Wordsy in front of the rest of us whether he'd seen Bonny, Wordsy said, 'Humankind cannot bear too much reality'. And that was all.

Just before my exams I started going down the Centre again. I recognised some of the faces and began getting back into it. The poetry circle hadn't been cancelled, it had just faded away. So one Wednesday evening I was down the Centre and the poster outside said: 'The Immortal and Versatile Sounds of Kool Skank, Hosted and Toasted by the Byron of Brixton, Bonny Lee'. I smiled to myself, because I knew who Byron was, but most of them youth, them wouldn't know. It just sounded good. The sounds were in the usual hall. The lights were turned down and the amplifier turned up and a jam of bodies presented itself as I went in.

For half an hour the music played, and Bonny's voice introduced the discs with a flourish. 'The latest creation of the Jamaican nation . . .' etc.

The bodies undulated. There was a thick smell of **ganja** about the room. 'Strike while the weed is hot . . .' Bonny shouted over the mike and he was greeted with catcalls and approving shouts. 'Go on, boy, fire some heavy shots, dread words 'pon the waves.' Then all of a sudden the record faded with a scratching sound. Some of the sounds-men gathered round the turntables with torches and began to put it right. 'Hold on there, hold a stool and keep your cool, brothers and sisters,' Bonny's voice announced over the mike. 'The emergency disco have hit an emergency in itself.'

The crowd was restless. They waited for a few minutes and then in the darkness they began to shout. They were threatening a stampede.

'Record player bust to boomber,' someone shouted.

The youth workers charged down from their office when they heard the commotion. They worked their way to the sounds table. There was an argument going on. The turntable had stopped functioning and the sounds-men were trying to figure it out, but the crowd wanted its sounds or it wanted its money back.

Then Bonny's voice came over the mike again. He was reciting some verses. They were his own verses and he read with a sort of threatening solemnity. Gradually the noise of the crowd, its protest, died down. People were listening.

'More,' they shouted when he'd finished his first poem.

---

ganja: marijuana

Bonny went through another, his voice reaching a higher pitch with excitement. Now the crowd was listening spellbound. 'Of bitter rain, my brothers y'all, of bitter rain, my sisters,' Bonny declared.

Then the record player was fixed and Bonny's **début** as a real poet was over. But when the record came on, the crowd shouted for more poetry. When the first record was over, another voice introduced Bonny again and a third and fourth and fifth poem boomed out over the amplifier.

After the session, Bonny waded his way through the crowd to the door. He saw me. He was sweating and his face shone with wet **elation**.

'I like it,' I said.

'Wha' go on there, Clyde?' he said.

'I there,' I replied and smiled.

Bonny and I stood outside the club and we talked of school and we talked of Wordsy. Bonny laughed and gave me a message for him.

I didn't give Wordsy the message. Then the day I was leaving school a black girl in the sixth form brought in a poster and pinned it to the notice board. It said: 'BONNY "BYRON" LEE', and it announced a poetry session by the 'Poet in Residence' at the Lambeth Library. There was a paragraph explaining that 'Byron' Lee had been given a grant by the Arts Council to work at 'black poetry and literature'.

Wordsy came into the room and his eye fell on the poster. 'So our friend Bonny's a professional poet,' he said to me.

---

début: first public appearance
elation: joyful excitement

'It would seem so,' I said.

'Do you ever see him?'

I told him I had and then, because he'd brought it up, I gave him Bonny's message.

'We was talking about you as a matter of fact,' I said, 'and he told me to tell you that he was wrong. That there aren't two kinds of truth. There's only one: Truth is what the masses like.'

'Hmm, that may be, that may very well be . . .' Wordsy said.

'But listen, he also said to thank you very much for being his teacher and showing him the ropes of poetry, Wordsworth and Eliot and Byron and all. He said he's been reading Wordsworth.'

'He didn't did he?' Wordsy said, his eyes lighting up.

'Yeah, that's what he said,' I lied.

Activities

Mr Mongoose and Mrs Hen by **James Berry**

Questions

1 Most of the first paragraph is happy and content. Find two adjectives that are used to convey this.

2 Pick out the words in the first paragraph that the writer uses to create a sense of suspense and approaching disaster.

3 In the first half of the story, what do you think of Mrs Ground-Dove's attitude to life – that Mrs Hen can do 'nothing' about what is happening to her?

4 Why does Mrs Hen believe that Mr Mongoose's actions will be punished?

5 'The court listened to Mrs Hen patiently. The court listened to her till she was completely finished.' The repetition in these lines is like the language of a children's story. This is not a children's story though, and the writer emphasises the words 'the court listened' for a different reason here. Why does he do this?

Activity

The words of Mrs Ground-Dove are central to this story. Early on in the tale we might think she is weak and gives up too quickly. By the end of the story we can understand why she feels so helpless even though it is important to fight for what you believe is right. These two activities focus on the allegorical meaning of the story:

- Find out what allegory is and write your own definition of it.
- There are many situations worldwide that involve unfairness and abuse of power. Write an allegorical story based on something you have read about on the news, for example the Stephen Lawrence case.

  Then write a paragraph explaining how your allegory relates to the issues in James Berry's story. You can search for the official government reports on the Stephen Lawrence Inquiry by title at: http://www.official-documents.co.uk. The most useful chapters are 1, 4 and 46.

*Note for teachers
The website above provides a useful resource for the classroom though the document is lengthy. Some sections are more accessible than others, and you may wish to select relevant information in order to differentiate within the group.

Further reading
If you enjoyed this you might like to read more of James Berry's short stories in *Thief in the village and other stories*. He has also written a lot of funny and lively poetry that you should be able to find in your school or local library.

The Loaded Dog by **Henry Lawson**

Questions

1 On pages 9–10 what are the differences between the characters of Andy and Dave in the way they usually work together?

2 What clues in the story show that these Australians are used to the outdoor life?

3 Look on page 14 at the section describing Dan and Jim running. Explain how the writer uses words to create a sense of breathless panic and speed. Look at the length of the sentences, the punctuation and the verbs he chooses.

4 Why do Dave, Jim and Andy all run in the same direction, following each other?

Activity

In the first few pages of the story, the writer describes Andy's construction of the bomb in great detail. Read the descriptions carefully and then, using imperative verbs (e.g. take . . ., cut . . .), construct your own step-by-step instructions for fishermen on how to blow up a fish that has stung you. You might like to add illustrations to help your reader. The first point has been done for you:

Step one: Take some blasting powder and place it in a skin of strong calico or canvas.

Further reading

If you enjoyed this story, try another of Henry Lawson's stories called *The Story of Malachi*. You will find it in his short-story collection *While the Billy Boils* in the Australian electronic text section of http://setix.library.usyd.edu.au. This is a disturbing story about bullying.

Attila by **R.K. Narayan**

Questions

1 What does the very first sentence of this story tell us about the dog?

2 Why do the family want a dog?

3 The writer creates comedy in the story by describing the dog as if he is human. The proper name for this technique is anthropomorphism. Can you find any examples of this on pages 21–22?

4 Can you think of a name that would be appropriate for Attila in the middle of the story and Attila the hero at the end of the story?

5 What does the expression 'to put someone on a pedestal' mean?

6 Can you explain what the last line of the story means? Why would Attila himself disagree with the mother's words?

Activity

Write a newspaper report on the burglary and Attila's role as the cunning detective. As you plan the article, you might like to consider the following elements:

- an eye-catching headline
- the facts of the story: when, where, why, what and who
- interviews with members of the family, the police or witnesses in the market place.

Further reading

If you enjoyed this story and would like to read more of R.K. Narayan's writing, you will find short stories in his collections *Malgudi Days* and *Under the Banyan Tree*. Another excellent book about a boy and his relationship with animals is *Cry of the Wolf* by Melvin Burgess.

Sredni Vashtar by **Saki**

Questions

1 The second paragraph of the story shows how Conradin finds pleasure in life. Explain in your own words how he does this.

2 The writer describes Conradin's surroundings, using adjectives to reflect how depressing his home life is. Pick out three adjectives in paragraph three and comment on how they create a depressing mood.

3 Who is 'the Woman', and why is a capital letter used here?

4 The writer, rather shockingly, uses the language of religion and prayer to describe Conradin's attitude to the ferret. Pick out the words and phrases in the story that are linked to religion on pages 30 and 33. Why do you think Saki uses these words and concepts in this way?

5 Comment on the last line of the story. Do you think it is a good ending? What does it show about the boy?

Activity

Conradin's imagination suggests that the Woman is killed by the power of Sredni Vashtar and his prayers, or rather curses. Poetry is often used for charms and curses because it uses words in a powerful way. Look at the Witches' spell from the beginning of Shakespeare's *Macbeth*, part of which is given below:

'Double double toil and trouble
Fire burn and cauldron bubble
Scale of dragon, tooth of wolf
Witches' mummy, maw and gulf
Of the ravin'd salt-sea shark,
Root of hemlock digg'd i' the dark . . .
Cool it with a baboon's blood
Then the charm is firm and good.'

Make up your own charm or curse for a particular purpose; for example a charm to cure someone of an illness, or a curse to make it rain. Think carefully about the language and images you choose and how they fit in with the purpose of your charm.

Further reading

If you enjoyed this story, try reading some of Saki's other stories: *The Open Window, Mrs Packletide's Tiger* and *The Mouse* at: http://www.bnl.com/shorts/.

First Foot by **Janice Galloway**

Questions

1 What does the first half of the story tell you about how the girl feels about her family?

2 From what the story tells you, what possible reasons could there be for the mother's irritation with the girl (page 39)?

3 From his actions and what is said about him, what sort of friend do you think Joe is? Use evidence from the text to support your answer.

4 The present that the girl has brought for her mother is not just a gift, but stands for more than that. Why is it so important to her that her mother should accept her present?

5 'I'm trapped with my own speechlessness.' (page 44). Why is the girl lost for words near the end of the story? What does she want to explain to her mother at this point?

Activity

This story focuses on adults and teenagers not understanding each other. At the beginning of the story we see that the girl's mother is upset and tired at her daughter's lack of communication and the fact that she is hardly ever at home.

- In a group, discuss what type of young people's behaviour might puzzle and irritate adults. Draw on your own experience of adults and teenagers.
- Imagine you are a parent finding their teenager difficult. Write a letter to the problem page of a magazine about your problem with your teenager. Swap your letter with another member of the class and answer their problem as if you are the agony aunt.

Further reading

If you enjoyed this story and would like to read a good novel about the relationships between teenagers and adults, try *Buddy* by Nigel Hinton.

Urban Myths: *The Choking Alsatian* **and** *The Vanishing Hitchhiker*

Questions

1 While more traditional myths and legends are set in the days of long ago, and 'once upon a time', urban legends are set in realistic, everyday places. How does the setting of each of these stories fit in with this rule?

2 Consider how suspense gradually builds up in *The Choking Alsatian*. In the description of the vet's telephone conversation, what clues are given that something strange has happened?

3 Can you think of similar clues that you could add to *The Vanishing Hitchhiker* to create suspense?

Activity

You can see that the first urban myth here has been adapted and lengthened to make the story spooky and interesting for the listener.

• Can you reduce the story of *The Choking Alsatian* to its most basic form, in twelve sentences, like *The Vanishing Hitchhiker*?

• Identify which parts of *The Vanishing Hitchhiker* you could expand with description and detail to make it longer, relevant and interesting to an audience of your own local friends. Then write the sections of the story, taking care to use descriptive language that will really help your listener to think the story is real.

You might like to read out your versions to the rest of the class and consider who has managed to create setting and atmosphere well by their descriptive language.

Further reading

If you enjoyed this popular story, try books of urban myths, such as *Now That's What I Call Urban Myths* by Phil Healey and Rick Glanvill.

The Sniper by **Liam O'Flaherty**

Questions

1 What is a sniper? Support your answer with brief quotations from the text.

2 On page 51 the writer creates a setting that fits this story of suspense and danger. Which words and phrases in the first paragraph help to create the setting and atmosphere?

3 On page 53 the writer describes the armoured car as though it were alive. Find the phrases in the text that illustrate this. Why do you think the writer has chosen to do this?

4 One of the disturbing elements of this story is that the sniper seems to enjoy his work. Can you find any evidence for this in the text?

5 What do you think about the end of the story? What does the writer suggest about civil war?

Activity

The writer has chosen to use many very short sentences. Normally your English teachers would encourage you not to write like this all the time. Select a paragraph where you can see many short sentences. Rewrite it, adding conjunctions (*and*, *but* and so on) to join up some sentences. Then compare the two versions. Try reading them aloud. Why do you think the writer chose to write in the style he did?

Further reading

If you enjoyed this story, you might like to find out about the more recent political situation in Northern Ireland through the novels *Across the Barricades* and *Dark Shadows* by Joan Lingard.

The Friendship by **Mildred D. Taylor**

Questions

1 Why do the children's parents dislike the Wallace family?

2 The moment when Little Man puts his hand in the dirt is a powerful one. Why do you think he does this and how does he feel?

3 How does the writer show that the white men in the shop regard black people as second-class citizens?

4 Why should John Wallace be respectful to Mr Tom Bee? Why will he not show this respect in public?

5 Do you think Mr Tom Bee is a foolish or an admirable character? Give reasons for your answer.

6 Why do you think the story is called *The Friendship*?

Activity

Pick a person from the story and make five points to comment on their character. Write under the following categories for each point you make: characteristics, quotation, comment. An example for Tom Bee is done for you:

Characteristics	Quotation	Comment
Tom Bee is a determined man	'Mr Tom Bee squared his shoulders.'	This quotation shows that Tom Bee is prepared to argue with people for what he believes. He does this when John Wallace tells him off for not calling him Mister.

Further reading

If you enjoyed this story you might like to read more of Mildred D. Taylor's short stories in *The Friendship and other stories*, or try her novel *Roll of Thunder, Hear my Cry*.

The Mirror by **Eiko Kadono**

Questions

1 By describing Ariko's behaviour with her parents at the beginning of the story, the writer suggests that she is becoming a teenager. What typical teenage behaviour can you see her displaying at this point in the story?

2 What did the original reflection in the mirror think of the Ariko she saw?

3 Look carefully at the way the new girl behaves to the mother on pages 88–89. What does she do that is rude or disrespectful?

4 The girl in the story is 12 years old and becoming more aware of her appearance and of boys. What do you think the writer is saying about girls of 12 and 13 and the way they behave?

5 At the end of the story both sides of Ariko join together. How does the writer show that Ariko has become more mature?

Activity

The curious mirror was found in an antiques shop. Find a picture of an interesting object from a magazine that might be found in a bric-à-brac or antiques shop. Then either:

- Swap it with a partner and then write a story behind the object you have been given; or
- Imagine that you are the owner of a bric-à-brac shop. Prepare a persuasive sales talk for a customer to try to sell the strange object. Deliver your talk to your partner.

Further reading

If you enjoyed this story, an excellent book which focuses on a young girl and the lively stories that her friend makes up to sell the objects in the family antiques shop is *A Pack of Lies* by Geraldine McCaughrean. Another good story is Anne Fine's *The Book of the Banshee* which focuses on a boy's experience of his impossible teenage sister who is destroying the family with her adolescent behaviour.

Once Upon a Time by **Nadine Gordimer**

Questions

1 The first paragraph of the 'bedtime story' on page 110 reads like a fairy tale. Pick out any words or phrases that remind you of a children's story.

2 The writer chooses not to use speech marks for direct speech in the story. As a result the dialogue and action combine to make long and breathless sentences. Pick out two examples of such sentences and read them aloud. Explain how such sentences reflect the mood of the story.

3 What do you think about the way the family in the story treat other people?

4 Re-read the first paragraph of the story. What objects and arrangements do this family seem to think will make them live 'happily ever after'?

5 Nadine Gordimer combines fairy-tale language with tense and violent subject matter. What images of destruction and violence stay in your mind, having read this story.

6 Do you think there is any moral to this story? What do you think it is?

Activities

Find out about the history of apartheid in South Africa and the role of Nelson Mandela in its eventual overthrow. You may find information in your school library or on the Internet. Write a paragraph outlining the most important facts you have found out. Then write a paragraph explaining how this story reflects the effects of apartheid in South Africa.

Further reading

If you enjoyed reading this story, you might like to read more of Nadine Gordimer's stories in *Jump and other stories*. The stories are set in London, Mozambique and South Africa.

The First of my Sins by **Brian Friel**

Questions

1 Why is David embarrassed by his Uncle George in front of his friends?

2 What do the hyphens show us about the way David speaks and thinks in the line, 'Bless-me-father-for-I-have sinned . . .'?

3 List the things David has done that his mother thinks are sinful rather than just normal childish behaviour.

4 The writer does not tell the story chronologically, but jumps from the present of the story to the past, and back to the present. Can you pinpoint the lines in the story where these time changes happen? Why does the writer structure the story like this?

5 What kind of person is David's mother? Think of three words to describe her character and find evidence in the text to support them.

6 By the end of the story David has some understanding of what sin is. Why do you think he feels that telling his mother about Uncle George was a sin?

Activities

David's opinion of Uncle George gradually changes. Examine the character of Uncle George. What do you learn about him as the story develops? Support each point you make with evidence from the text.

Further reading

If you enjoyed this story you might like to read *Oliver Twist* by Charles Dickens, which also focuses on the experience of children being judged by adults, moral issues and petty crime.

The Guest by **Leena Dhingra**

Questions

1 What impression do you gain of the grandmother in the first three pages of the story?

2 What does Divya dislike about Mrs Collins when she first meets her?

3 What does Divya find difficult about Indian culture?

4 How does Divya feel when on page 142 she says: 'Wasn't it all just so sweet and cosy'?

5 How does Nani's hospitality change Mrs Collins?

6 Having read the end of the story, what would you say *The Guest* is about? Think of some alternative titles for the story.

Activities

'Life is full of lessons. And there is always more to learn.'
Write about one of the following:

- an account of a time when you realised something important or learned a lesson in life
- a story entitled 'Life is full of lessons'
- a person from whom you have learned a lot. Describe them and what they have taught you.

Further reading

If you enjoyed this story, look in your library for books by Jamilla Gavin which are set in India. You might like to try the brilliant adult book called *Anita and Me* by Meera Syal, about an Indian girl growing up in England.

Fifty-Fifty Tutti-Frutti Chocolate-Chip
by **Norman Silver**

Questions

1 Why is the burning of the medical book important to Basil?

2 Norman Silver writes this story in an informal way as if Basil is speaking to the reader directly. Pick out three examples of this. What effect does this have on the reader?

3 What do Basil's comments about Bonzo suggest about the police force in Cape Town?

4 Why do you think Basil uses the words 'coon' and 'coloured' about the black people in the story? Do you think the writer wants us to think badly of him?

5 Some people enjoy violent films and television programmes. In this story the writer makes it clear that Basil is shocked and disgusted by the violent behaviour of the white boys. Look closely at the language and identify particular words and phrases that show this.

6 What do you think about the end of the story? What does it show about Basil and the pressures he is under?

Activities

Write Basil's rejected 'penetrating' article for a newspaper or a magazine' on the events of the story. Either write his version of them, or a rewritten version that might be acceptable to a newspaper read by the white people of Cape Town.

Think about including:

- a headline
- interviews with witnesses
- police reports
- the five essential elements of a newspaper story: who, what, why, when and where.

Further reading

If you enjoyed this story, you might like to read Norman Silver's novels *No Tigers in Africa* and *Python Dance*. Robert Swindell's *Smash* is another excellent story about racial prejudice and violence.

Two Kinda Truth by **Farrukh Dhondy**

Questions

1 Irving tells the story using his own dialect. Pick three examples of this non-standard English and rewrite the sentences in standard English.

2 Why do the boys tease Wordsy at the beginning of the story?

3 What do you learn about Wordsy's teaching methods during the story? What do you think is effective about his way of teaching and what would you criticise?

4 What does Wordsy mean by 'Humankind cannot bear too much reality'?

5 What is the significance of the title *Two Kinda Truth* and how does it relate to the end of the story?

Activity

This story focuses on the form of poetry called performance poetry.

• Research the famous Rastafarian performance poet Benjamin Zephaniah in your school library or on the Internet. Write a paragraph on his life and find one poem by him that you would like to share with the class.

• Bonny's rap poem is about political issues and the experience of black people. Find a current issue in the newspaper and write your own rhyming rap poem about it in the style of Bonny or Zephaniah.

Further reading

If you enjoyed this story you might like to read some other short stories by Farrukh Dhondy. The stories in *Come to Mecca and other stories* are all set in multi-racial inner-city areas and are gripping and often disturbing tales.

Extended writing activities

1 Compare and contrast the portrayal of the family and growing up in *The Mirror* by Eiko Kadono and *The Guest* by Leena Dhingra. Write your introduction to the stories and then use some of the sentence starters below to write your essay. Remember to use quotations from the text to support your points.

- The settings of the stories are very different.
- The central female characters in the two stories are different ages: Divya is clearly more grown-up than Ariko.
- Both stories address the theme of friendship.
- Both stories address the theme of growing up.
- Both stories portray the family and the relationships between adults and young people.
- *The Guest* is written in the first person and *The Mirror* is written in the third person. The effect of this is that . . .
- The stories both end with the central characters having matured through their experiences and learned something about themselves and other people.
- The story I prefer is . . . My reasons are . . .

2 Compare and contrast *The Friendship* by Mildred D. Taylor and *Fifty-Fifty Tutti-Frutti Chocolate-Chip* by Norman Silver. Plan your essay by writing notes on some of the following aspects of both stories and then use the bullet points to structure your essay. Remember to select quotations from the texts to support your opinions:

- a brief introduction to each story
- the first-person narration
- setting
- memorable characters
- events in the story
- cultural background
- the writer's use of language
- the attitude of the writer
- which story you prefer and why.

Routeway

The routeway below outlines some suggestions of focus for further study. The list is by no means exhaustive, but outlines the principal links between stories by both topics and literary method.

Story	Topics/Literary methods
Mr Mongoose and Mrs Hen	Racism
	The oral tradition
	Social/historical background
	Children's stories
The Loaded Dog	Humour
	Animals
Attila	India
	Humour
	Twist in the tale
	Animals
Sredni Vashtar	Ritual
	Adult/child relationships
	Fear and horror
First Foot	Teenage experience
	Friendship
	First-person narration
	Ritual
	Adult/child relationships
Urban Myths	The oral tradition
	Twist in the tale
	Fear and horror
The Sniper	Twist in the tale
	Social/historical background
	Use of style and language to support meaning

Story	Topics/Literary methods
The Friendship	Racism
	Friendship
	Adult/child relationships
	Violence
	First-person narration
The Mirror	Teenage experience
	Adult/child relationships
Once Upon a Time	Racism
	Use of style and language to support meaning
	Social/historical background
	South Africa
	Twist in the tale
The First of my Sins	Judging others
	Adult/child relationships
	Ritual
	First-person narration
The Guest	Friendship
	Judging others
	India
	First-person narration
	A meeting of different cultures
Fifty-Fifty Tutti-Frutti Chocolate-Chip	Different perspectives
	South Africa
	Social/historical background
	Teenage experience
	Adult/child relationships
	First-person narration
	Violence
Two Kinda Truth	Friendship
	First-person narration
	Racism
	Different perspectives

Heinemann
New Windmills

Founding Editors: Anne and Ian Serraillier

Chinua Achebe Things Fall Apart
David Almond Skellig
Maya Angelou I Know Why the Caged Bird Sings
Margaret Atwood The Handmaid's Tale
Jane Austen Pride and Prejudice
Stan Barstow Joby: A Kind of Loving
Nina Bawden Carrie's War; The Finding; Humbug
Malorie Blackman Tell Me No Lies; Words Last Forever
Charlotte Brontë Jane Eyre
Emily Brontë Wuthering Heights
Melvin Burgess and Lee Hall Billy Elliot
Betsy Byars The Midnight Fox; The Pinballs; The Eighteenth Emergency
Victor Canning The Runaways
Sir Arthur Conan Doyle Sherlock Holmes Short Stories
Susan Cooper King of Shadows
Robert Cormier Heroes
Roald Dahl Danny; The Champion of the World; The Wonderful Story of Henry Sugar; George's Marvellous Medicine; The Witches; Boy; Going Solo; Matilda; My Year
Anita Desai The Village by the Sea
Charles Dickens A Christmas Carol; Great Expectations; A Charles Dickens Selection
Berlie Doherty Granny was a Buffer Girl; Street Child
Roddy Doyle Paddy Clarke Ha Ha Ha
George Eliot Silas Marner
Anne Fine The Granny Project
Leon Garfield Six Shakespeare Stories
Ann Halam Dr Franklin's Island
Thomas Hardy The Withered Arm and Other Wessex Tales; The Mayor of Casterbridge
Ernest Hemmingway The Old Man and the Sea; A Farewell to Arms
Barry Hines A Kestrel For A Knave
Nigel Hinton Buddy; Buddy's Song
Anne Holm I Am David

Janni Howker Badger on the Barge; The Nature of the Beast; Martin Farrell
Pete Johnson The Protectors
Geraldine Kaye Comfort Herself
Daniel Keyes Flowers for Algernon
Dick King-Smith The Sheep-Pig
Elizabeth Laird Red Sky in the Morning
D H Lawrence The Fox and The Virgin and the Gypsy; Selected Tales
Harper Lee To Kill a Mockingbird
C Day Lewis The Otterbury Incident
Joan Linguard Across the Barricades
Penelope Lively The Ghost of Thomas Kemp
Geraldine McCaughrean Stories from Shakespeare; Pack of Lies
Bernard MacLaverty Cal; The Best of Bernard MacLaverty
Jan Mark Heathrow Nights
James Vance Marshall Walkabout
Ian McEwan The Daydreamer; A Child in Time
Michael Morpurgo The Wreck of the Zanzibar; Why the Whales Came; Arthur, High King of Britain; Kensuke's Kingdom; From Hereabout Hill; Robin of Sherwood
Beverley Naidoo No Turning Back; The Other Side of Truth
Bill Naughton The Goalkeeper's Revenge
New Windmill A Charles Dickens Selection
New Windmill Anthology of Challenging Texts: Thoughtlines
New Windmill Book of Classic Short Stories
New Windmill Book of Fiction and Non-fiction: Taking Off!
New Windmill Book of Greek Myths
New Windmill Book of Haunting Tales
New Windmill Book of Humorous Stories: Don't Make Me Laugh
New Windmill Book of Nineteenth Century Short Stories
New Windmill Book of Non-fiction: Get Real
New Windmill Book of Non-fiction: Real Lives, Real Times
New Windmill Book of Scottish Short Stories
New Windmill Book of Short Stories: Fast and Curious
New Windmill Book of Short Stories: From Beginning to End
New Windmill Book of Short Stories: Into the Unknown
New Windmill Book of Short Stories: Tales with a Twist
New Windmill Book of Short Stories: Trouble in Two Centuries
New Windmill Book of Short Stories: Ways with Words
New Windmill Book of Stories from Many Cultures and Traditions; Fifty-Fifty Tuti-Fruity Chocolate Chip

How many have you read?